MIRRORS

HUNTER BUREAU #1

BLAZE WARD

KNOTTED ROAD PRESS

Hunter Bureau

Mirrors

Latency

The Handsome Rob Gigs

Can't Shoot Straight Gang

Can't Shoot Straight Gang Returns

Hunting Handsome Rob

Handsome Rob, Assassin

The Jessica Keller Chronicles

Auberon

Queen of the Pirates

Last of the Immortals

Goddess of War

Flight of the Blackbird

The Red Admiral

St. Legier

Winterhome

Petron

CS-405

Queen Anne's Revenge

Packmule

Persephone

Additional Alexandria Station Stories

Siren

Two Bottles of Wine with a War God

The Story Road

The Science Officer Series

The Science Officer

The Mind Field

The Gilded Cage

The Pleasure Dome

The Doomsday Vault

The Last Flagship

The Hammerfield Gambit

The Hammerfield Payoff

Shadow of the Dominion

Longshot Hypothesis

Hard Bargain

Outermost

Dominion-427

Phoenix

Princess Rualoh

Mirrors
Hunter Bureau #1
Blaze Ward
Copyright © 2020 Blaze Ward
All rights reserved
Published by Knotted Road Press
www.KnottedRoadPress.com

ISBN: 978-1-64470-175-1

Cover art:

ID 131408614 © Andrey Golubtsov | Dreamstime.com
ID 96424818 © Ilya Shalkov | Dreamstime.com

Cover and interior design copyright © 2020 Knotted Road Press

Reviews
It's true. Reviews help. Even a short one, such as, "Loved it!" So please consider reviewing this book (and all of the ones you've read) on your favorite retailer site.

Never miss a release!
If you'd like to be notified of new releases, sign up for my newsletter.

http://www.blazeward.com/newsletter/

Buy More!
Did you know that you can buy directly from my website?

https://www.blazeward.com/shop/

[1]

SUNSET

Greyson couldn't remember it ever raining this much when he was a kid, but forty years had a way of coating everything over with a pretty glaze that covered up all the nicks and burns of living. At least it was a cool rain this afternoon, a thick, misty drizzle that just kind of smeared the dirt and soot around, rather than beating you down bodily and driving you to your knees, like the kid at the end of those romantic vids, right before the girl appears out of the downpour and they both live happily ever after.

Or whatever came after the credits rolled. Greyson was still trying to figure that one out himself.

Weather was supposed to get really ugly later today, according to the folks paid to know these things. Hotter and wetter, but he figured to be back indoors by then, with a highball of synth whiskey in one hand and some classical music on the box. Let the weirdos who liked rain and any handy, aquatic, alien life forms have it.

Weather Control was still mostly a crap shoot, even with the aliens helping, but when they promised it would get

1

worse, Greyson tended to believe them. Even with aliens like the Mooz helping, scientists hadn't been able to undo all the damage humans had done to their home world, but it had only been fifteen years since everyone arrived, and some things took time, even for space wizards, or whatever the *Illymus Merchant Guild* was.

They claimed they could fix it given time, but he'd probably be dead by then anyway, so Greyson just dealt with it and kept his head down. Quiet life and all that.

Greyson didn't have to live as cheap as he did, but a lifetime's habits get too deeply ingrained for most people to break, and he hadn't found any reason to yet. This afternoon, that meant udon noodles in a hot broth, with vat-grown shrimp tossed in for protein, down at the corner joint where the owner was American-Born-Chinese and didn't stint on the noodles much.

These days, most people lived dreary, bargain-priced lives. Cheap, synth whiskey. Genengineered shrimp. Noodle shops like this with four, tiny tables, open in front to the rain but dry, as long as the wind stayed calm and didn't start swirling in among the mighty tower flats above him.

If it did change, he'd adapt. Greyson was good at that. He'd been US Army once upon a time. Until the aliens announced that large, standing military forces were unacceptable and forced everybody to demobilize down to defensive forces and local National Guard units. Hadn't really impacted the sorts of special forces things he'd been doing prior to that, but lots of other people were suddenly out of work.

Greyson would have said the world went to hell, but it was already there, so a decade-long recession hadn't done much to make it worse. The aliens had at least brought cash to invest in art and roads, and shipped in food when too many people might have starved.

You didn't argue with people like that. Just listened when they said they had your best interests at heart, nodded in the appropriate conversational lulls, and got on with your life.

That meant it was only sort of weird to realize the person at the next table behind you was actually a G'schtack and not a Human. Hard to tell at first glance, but Greyson had been a cop for a while after he was done being a soldier, and those things came natural.

Skin a little too gray. Bald head, but natural, rather than age or shaving it. Ears a little low under that bowler hat, and stuck out wider than even in the old cartoons.

If he felt like getting up, he could have walked around the front of the guy to confirm, but he knew a G'schtack when he saw one. They looked the closest to Humans anyway. And knowing was just part of the job.

Detective/Hunter Greyson Leigh. Earth Police Special Missions.

The Hunter Bureau.

The humans who went after bad aliens.

He didn't do that anymore, so he didn't really care if the guy over there slurping his own udon was a gun runner, a hophead, or an anthropologist doing field work. As long as the man didn't bother a guy and his noodles.

The shadow that just appeared out of the mist was going to be enough of a bother, probably for both of them.

Short. Fat. Bald.

You could fix two of the three these days with a little chemistry, but Zielinski wasn't that kind of guy. Doing that would have required an admission that there was something wrong with the man in the first place.

Something external, anyway.

Detective/Captain Olek Jan Zielinski. Commander, Eastern North America Division, Earth Police Special Missions.

Dressed like a civilian, in a badly-fit, off-the-rack suit that had possibly been considered stylish forty years ago when the man most likely bought it. Brown slacks. Darker jacket. Pale green shirt buttoned up under a black tie. Went together about as well as the man did.

Greyson felt a rumbly sigh and went back to his noodles. At least lunch wasn't going to give him any grief.

He didn't do hats, so he didn't have one to pull down over his eyes as camouflage, not that it probably would have mattered as the man approached.

"Leigh."

The voice hadn't gotten any better. Still a bad wheeze mixed with rusty iron shavings. Maybe the nickel shavings you tossed into hydrochloric acid to create a chemical gas that ate people's lungs quick enough if you felt like being an asshole.

Like Zielinski.

Greyson looked up and continued to suck down a noodle like a worm trying to escape justice. He grunted vaguely.

Zielinski took that as invitation and sat down across the small table from him.

The owner behind the counter started to say something, but the cop turned a hard glare on him, the kind that promised health inspectors with an attitude problem, and the man subsided.

Greyson studied his old boss while he retained his personal space.

"You're a hard man to find," Zielinski grunted. "It's like you didn't want anybody from the old days coming around."

"And yet, here you are," Greyson cocked his head slightly, as if studying the man.

Trying out various insults in his head to see if he could find the one that fit best.

The cop had gotten older in the last year and a half. More lines carved into that round face. Fewer wisps of gray hair on top of his pate.

"Got a job for you, Leigh," the short, fat cop tried to at least sound friendly.

Greyson considered the man briefly, sat his bowl down in the middle of the table, and took a sip of the tea that was too thin and already nearly ambient temperature.

"Not a cop anymore, Zielinski," he replied laconically. "Little people now."

It was an old joke. You were big people, with a badge and a gun, or nobody. Measure of that man's opinion of the teeming masses of humanity, and the hundred thousand or so aliens living at least temporarily on Earth these days.

"We could fix that, Leigh," the man tried to put on a sociable face. Fit him like a cheap Halloween mask. "Bring you back."

"You're the one who fired me, Olek," Greyson fixed a distant glare on the man.

"We all make mistakes, Greyson," the shorter cop replied, still trying to be cozy.

"And then Dominguez showed up at my apartment three days later," Greyson continued, as if the man hadn't spoken a word. "Waited until I had opened the door to upend a box of the few personal items you hadn't already trashed or burned. Dumped them in the hallway with your compliments, specifically, and walked away laughing. You know how Dominguez sounds when he laughs."

"Somebody had to take the fall for that one," the man finally seemed to give up on friendliness and let anger peek out. "You screwed up and the Chief Commissioner decided she'd had enough of your attitude problems."

"I'll try to keep in mind that enforcing the law can be

problematical around folks like you and your friends, Zielinski," Greyson offered dryly, picking his bowl back up and adjusting his sticks just so.

He could tell how anxious the man must be by the mere fact that he hadn't stormed off already. Or flipped the table into Greyson's lap. Or punched him in the face.

They must be desperate.

The silence stretched a little.

"You don't need me. Remember?" Greyson decided to stick a few hot needles under fingernails when the man still hadn't gone away.

He couldn't remember where he'd heard the phrase, but it fit in a lovely way.

"We got a *freak* loose, Leigh," Zielinski sputtered. "Somehow got past the border checks without a shift-blocker on, or snuck here. Butchering people and absorbing their memories. Serial killer. The kind of thing the Hunter Bureau was created to stop."

Freak.

Zielinski never called the species by their correct name. Never said *Phrenic.* Only *freak.*

But Olek Zielinski was also the kind of cop that forty-odd years later still referred to a President of the United States of America as "*that nigger.*"

Hated everyone that didn't look like him. Didn't talk like him. If you weren't Polack-American from Chicago, you were trash. Adding a bunch of alien species to the mix just meant that many more kinds of people for him to insult and abuse. Colors and shapes beyond all the humans the man could oppress.

Zielinski hated them all.

It had probably been his calling in life to join and help shape the Hunter Bureau when it got started. Greyson assumed CPD had been happy to get rid of the man and all the problems an attitude like that probably brought to the concept of community policing. He was an iron hammer when most of the time you needed a velvet glove.

But what did that make Greyson Leigh? The army had taught him to kill efficiently and remorselessly. After twenty years and a pension, he became a cop. One of the good guys, he kept telling himself when he needed to sleep.

Detective/Hunter Greyson Leigh. A professional killer that supposedly only did in the bad guys. Or had, back when he had a job.

Army pension was enough, if you lived frugal. Plus he had other money saved up to go with what little pension the Bureau left him with. Never married and never bought himself a fancy car or rocketbike when he was a kid. Lived quiet. Synth whiskey and classical music.

Greyson let his introspective moment fade and fixed a hard, angry glare on the cop across the table.

"You don't need my kind around, messing things up. That's what you said," he snarled in a compact voice that the G'schtack over there might hear only because the species had good ears. "Dominguez always said he could do my job better than I could. Send him. Or Kovalchuk. They're your boys, Captain."

"Kovalchuk's dead," the captain growled back. "Got killed by a Dyarnan art thief serving a warrant about six months ago."

"And Dominguez?" Greyson prodded.

"The *freak* got him last week, Leigh," Zielinski's voice suddenly got low and fierce as well. "That's how we know what we're facing. Thing broke his neck and was just about to suck his brains out when Asher chased it off. Might have wounded it, but she didn't have a cannon for killing a *skinwalker*, so it probably just found a dark corner and healed itself."

Greyson nodded. Killing an adult Phrenic not wearing a shift-blocker required a nerve scrambler at medium range or closer. Bureau didn't issue them to officers in the field, since a palmstunner worked on just about everyone else and wasn't immediately lethal if you had to shoot wildly into a crowd.

The Articles of Acceptance into the Illymus Merchant Guild specified that most crimes were not punished capitally, regardless of human preferences, so even killing folks while arresting them was itself a crime. Most aliens were deported and served a short stint in an off-planet prison camp somewhere.

Rogue Phrenic who had come here without a shift-blocker, who could become anybody they touched long enough, were an entirely different situation.

Zielinski's term, *skinwalker*, was probably as accurate as anything else. Human sized. Human shaped, with two arms, two legs, torso, head with all the sensory apparatus in place.

Problems came because they could adapt themselves. Like chameleons. Change the their skin tone and texture. Grow hair that looked real enough. Even change their height and build a little as a way of becoming someone else.

One Greyson's size couldn't easily redo himself to look like the short, fat, ugly son of a bitch across the table, but with ten billion humans to pick from, you could hide anywhere pretty easily with a little patience.

That wouldn't be a problem, except for when Phrenic decided to become predators. Killed you, and then extruded tentacles from their face that let them absorb all your memories.

They didn't actually suck out your brains and eat them, but the image was similar enough. With all your memories, they could become you.

At least until they got bored. Or got a better offer.

Made them dangerous. Hard to find. Harder to stop.

Most of them weren't bad folk, which was why the Guild had never xenocided the lot. Invented the shift-blocker instead to keep them in their native form, at least until somebody came along with the tools to remove it.

They ate meat like other species, and law everywhere said it had to be below a certain level of intelligence to be a food animal. Dolphins were out. Cattle were just fine.

And Zielinski was sitting across the table from him, offering Greyson back his old job.

Because they needed a killer.

Fight fire with fire, or something similar.

"Why the hell do I care, Olek?" he asked in an exasperated tone as his noodle bowl was finally empty.

If they were this serious, Greyson could probably just run this as long as he wanted, rubbing the bastard's nose in it.

"You were the best, Greyson," the cop finally climbed down off his lofty superiority to admit some truth to the conversation. Maybe bend that stiff neck a little.

He had been the best. Not the best killer. That had probably been Jansen. No, he had been the best cop. The best *Hunter*. Find the trail and track the beast back to its lair, where you could take it in or take it down with the least risk of casualties.

Do justice, instead of the sort of violence that men like Jansen or Zielinski used. Scalpel, not maul.

"Past tense, Zielinski," Greyson noted. "Retired now. Got a pension. Considering maybe trying one of the off-world colonies. See the galaxy. That sort of thing. Put my past behind me."

The last bit he lofted at the man in a cold, dry tone, like a Yanagiba knife going after fresh otoro.

"I got a serial killer *freak* loose on the streets of the Eastern Metroplex, pal," Zielinski was starting to lose his temper finally. And most of the profanity had vanished from his working vocabulary.

Must have gone to see someone about anger issues and actually listened to them for once. Didn't used to take this much effort to get under the man's skin.

"Isn't that what the Hunter Bureau was formed for, Zielinski?" Greyson asked. "Find aliens you don't like and kill them?"

The G'schtack had either finally started paying attention to the conversation, or maybe just heard enough. He rose now in a graceful motion, scowled at the two of them as he adjusted his derby hat on a bald skull, and walked into the wall of mist lurking just beyond the awning.

"Hey, you, too, punk," Zielinski snarled after the alien in an ugly voice, but that was just the reflex of an old Chicago cop not letting anyone else have the last word. Even silently.

Zielinski's eyes turned back to his and took on a harder gleam.

"I could always force you to come back to duty," he said in a cruel, harsh tone.

Greyson couldn't help himself. The laughter bubbled up and erupted all over the place before he could control it.

Felt kinda nice, after the craziness of the last few days. Like he was almost back to normal from a cold, whatever normal was in this modern age with aliens and interstellar travel. Crap that had been science fiction when he was a kid.

Zielinski just glared. And waited. Greyson finally got his mirth under control.

"Sure," he said. "You try that, Zielinski. Drag me kicking and screaming into your office, threaten my life, my pension, and any friends I might have made. And then hand me a nerve scrambler big enough to take down a Phrenic. *I dare you.*"

Something finally registered in those brown eyes. Fear, maybe. Greyson Leigh had never been one for idle threats.

Idle anything, when he thought about it. Even his synth whiskey and classical music were approached with a scholarly bent. An old philosopher keeping his wits sharp by expanding his mind.

He could have taken up chess, but that was too dry and mathematical, just studying the old masters and their famous games. Better to step onto a board with ten thousand options and whole symphonies to explore them.

Zielinski apparently finally thought better of stupid threats.

Or making a man like Greyson Leigh angry and then handing him a weapon capable of shattering a human mind forever.

Man who didn't have much of a life might not have much to lose, copper.

"What will it take to get you to come back in harness?" Zielinski finally asked.

Greyson should have known that they'd have to go through the whole Kubler-Ross pattern of grief. Man like Zielinski couldn't work it all out in his head yesterday and start the conversation at the end.

No, he had to drag Greyson down the damned path, one ugly stone at a time.

Now we've made it as far as Bargaining.

Greyson studied the man. Saw the tiny soul that made a good political cop, where there were no ethics that would prevent him from rising as far as his violence, grudges, and racism could take him. Probably should call it specism these days, since Zielinski didn't stop at just hating Blacks, Hispanics, Jews, and Asians. He had whole new species to hate as well.

What the hell.

"Your head, on the proverbial stick, Olek," Greyson said simply. "You want me back, you retire and someone else takes over this office."

"Think they'll offer you my job, punk?" Olek snarled. "Is that what this is all about?"

"I don't want your job, Zielinski," Greyson countered. "The Commission couldn't offer me enough to take it. I just think you're an asshole that makes things worse, not better. Plus you're a corrupt son of a bitch who protects guilty people for a bribe. That's why you and the Commissioner fired me in the first place, remember? I busted too many of your buddies. Probably cost you enough income that you had to give up a couple of your mistresses. At least until I was gone."

The man was seething. Greyson wondered if there was a way he could get to do this on a weekly basis, just for how much it improved his humor to take his anger out on a shit bird like Olek Jan Zielinski.

And still the man sat there, taking it. Must be under strict orders from the Commissioner to bring Greyson Leigh in from the cold, no matter what.

No matter what?

Greyson wondered if someone else was holding the Commissioner's feet to the fire as well.

Just how bad did they want him?

"And if I refuse?" Zielinski ground out the words like a stone mill making flour.

Greyson shrugged.

"I didn't ask you to come ruin my digestion, Captain," he sneered sharply. "You can go away and leave me in peace, any time you want."

"I got no more choice in this matter than you do, Leigh," the Detective/Captain of the Eastern North America Division, Earth Police Special Missions, Hunter Bureau admitted quietly. "The Commissioner's got no choice. The Brass demanded the best. Ordered him to get you on the case. Whatever the cost."

Greyson nodded, inwardly appalled at how high up the food chain that sort of command must have originated. Earth Police didn't answer to many people. That was the nature of the beast.

"Well, you go tell them my price, Olek," Greyson said in a friendlier tone. "You for me. See what she says about that. You know how to find me now."

Rather than wait for an answer, Greyson Leigh stood up and stepped away from the table. The mist wasn't bad. His longcoat would keep most of it off of him, and he flipped the collar up to keep it off the back of his neck.

Wasn't that far to his apartment, and a glass of synth whiskey and some classical music.

Glancing back, Olek Zielinski hadn't moved, other than to track Greyson with his hard, cop eyes.

Greyson smiled and walked into the mist.

There was a moment of discontinuity as Greyson walked away, as though he faded and someone else took up residence in his body.

One soul, shifted to the side for another.

Ethen looked out of Greyson's eyes and wondered.

Zaborra had been right. Absorbing Greyson Leigh's life had been the best way to make sure they would never be found. Ethen didn't know how long he could go on pretending to be the man, especially in light of today, but Ethen had been under strict orders from Zaborra, and he'd never been one to argue when people raised their voices.

The rain absorbed him, like he had Greyson. At least the cops would never call his bluff. Never toss Zielinski onto the trash heap of history to bring Greyson Leigh back onto the force. Another few days, maybe a week, and Ethen could escape this dangerously-smart cop in his mind and find someone else to impersonate.

Someone who didn't judge him so harshly when they were alone. Didn't whisper *loser* when they slept.

But Ethen had no idea how to escape.

14

GREYSON JOLTED AWAKE WITH A START, NOT QUITE SURE where he was. The room was his apartment, a compact studio on the seventh floor of a tower in what used to be the old American city of Boston. Back before it all got consolidated into the larger Eastern Metroplex, this one, ongoing city ranging all the way down to what used to be the District of Columbia when people still lived in the middle of the country.

Before things got too weird there.

And before the aliens showed up.

The sound returned. The one that had jarred him out of wherever it was he had been before. Classical music still emanated from the brass and glass machine on the end table. A highball glass of synth whiskey was still in his left hand, unspilled, so he hadn't been gone for long, wherever he had been.

Someone was knocking at his door.

Greyson Leigh didn't have friends. Not like other humans.

Ethen Boli knew this. He had killed the cop and stolen

his form and his memories nearly a week ago, as a way of hiding on this planet.

Hiding from the Hunters. The other Hunters.

He was Greyson Leigh these days, except he wasn't. He had to be, though, because Zaborra had been right. The *Illymus Merchant Guild* had told the human authorities that they had at least one Phrenic killer loose on this planet. The humans had called in the Hunter Bureau, the one police force on the planet capable of stalking a rogue *Phrenic* shapeshifter through whatever transformation he might take in an attempt to flee justice.

To escape men like Greyson Leigh.

A third knock. Whoever it was would not be going away. Ethen realized that he had previously turned the music up during a section of Beethoven's Ninth that Greyson particularly liked, the *Ode To Joy*, and whoever it was outside could hear that.

Would know that the person imitating Greyson Leigh was present.

Panic grabbed Ethen by the throat. Fear that he might have to kill someone to protect himself, when he wasn't even sure he could do that anymore. Wasn't sure how to deal with that cop's eye staring back at him in the mirror.

He rose slowly, calling on Greyson's memories to try to guess who might have come. It was too soon for more police to try to convince him to accept *unretirement*. The Detective/Captain of the regional Hunter Bureau, that asshole Zielinski, would have to pass the word up a convoluted chain of humans to reach one that could order all the lessers to give way in spite of the risk to their petty corruptions.

That had been Zaborra's fallback. The bluff that would make the cops settle on a lesser Hunter than Greyson Leigh.

Someone not good enough to find them before they could escape again.

Ethen didn't understand why. He just did what he was told.

Ethen approached the door, fervently locking himself into the form of Greyson Leigh, former Detective/Hunter, and put an eye to the peephole. It was a measure of how old this building was that they still used a fisheye lens made of glass to see through a closed door, rather than installing a camera.

But then, Greyson had been a frugal man in life. No exorbitant expenses, even when he could have afforded them in his youth. Army pension and good savings. Cheap living and inexpensive udon noodles with vat-grown shrimp, rather than steak.

The form outside had a name, when Ethen looked.

Emelina Antúnez.

Emmy.

A mind of hot-forged steel, honed by business to an edge capable of severing limbs with a flick. wrapped around an amazingly beautiful, muscular body. The kind that saw the Argentinian Tango as a warm-up for serious dancing.

She had a smell that Ethen could suddenly remember. A taste as well, something unlike anything a Phrenic had ever consumed. Something that caused his heart to start pounding with a different kind of energy than the fear he had lived with for over a week.

He could not merely ignore the woman. He would, in fact, need her as part of his charade, if he was to pass himself off convincingly as the very cop the humans were going to send to track him and Zaborra down.

But Ethen understood that he could not afford a single mistake in front of her either. Greyson knew she had broken lesser men with her will and passion. Ethen was not her equal. Very few intelligent beings were, human or not. Greyson Leigh was apparently one of them.

Frightening, but he had already known what kind of man Greyson was, and was doing his best not to embarrass the man's memory.

There was one thing he could do. It was a desperate, risky maneuver. If he failed, he would have to destroy the entire situation and go back to running for his life. Ethen had never tried it before, but he had no choice now.

It was *Emmy* on his doorstep.

Nothing could derail this woman, if she scented danger or lies.

He stepped back inside himself and let Greyson Leigh take charge of their body.

———

GREYSON OPENED THE DOOR AND SMILED AT EMMY. Gods, no woman should be allowed to look that good.

Her comm chirped and she held up a hand as she answered it, letting him just drink her in while she negotiated some new deal.

Tall and dusky. Mexican parents, originally, but pureblood Spanish on both sides. Brown hair bobbed just long enough to grab hold of in one hand and pull. Dark eyes that didn't miss anything. Body that just didn't stop. Flowery sun-dress clinging in the right places, reminding you she didn't have anything on under it.

Didn't need anything.

Greyson only had a decade on the woman, but she could run boys fresh out of boot camp into the ground when she wanted.

Her voice rose in anger, directed at someone else. Something about points on the back plus contingencies and escape clauses. Greyson couldn't really follow it, but someone was getting a tongue-lashing. The bad kind.

"Good," she finally announced as Greyson smelled the musk of Emmy's power wafting across the room. "Deliver that in a contract form to my office tonight. I'll read it at dawn, redline where you screwed anything up, and send it back. Clear your lunch so we can get it signed and notify the bank that I'll need up to seventy-five million in cash for closing."

She paused, turning finally back to study him with eyes that seemed dangerous enough to read all his secrets.

"Yes," she jabbed at someone on the comm. "Seventy-five. I might need to grind them down a few million when I see the Mumbai opening, or offer another tenth on the back for some up-front. This is a deal for a lot of money, so everyone needs to be happy before we move on to Wallerstone next. Questions? Okay, execute it and remind me why I put up with your exorbitant billing rates, Danzer."

She closed the comm and slipped it into a pocket. Even her clothing wrapped around her like a dancer, tight here and sliding there, just to show off those muscles and lines.

Predator on the prowl. Greyson felt like prey.

"I was beginning to think you had another woman in there," she said, moving to the threshold and leaning against the door jamb as he moved back, a knowing grin on her face as she glanced over his shoulder. Seduction emanated from every pore like lilacs, laying over the musk of whatever deal she'd just done.

"She went out the fire escape," Greyson grinned with a twinkle in his eyes, stepping to one side. "Apparently, I got the calendar messed up again and almost had two of you at once."

Emmy kissed him on the cheek then stepped past him

into the flat with an extra wiggle to her bottom under that flowery sun dress, entering his existence irrevocably.

"Threesome might be fun sometime," she glanced back over a shoulder with a lascivious grin.

"Sure," Greyson said as he closed the door and set the deadbolt. "If I had a death wish or something. You're almost too much for me to handle all by yourself. Get you a drink?"

Emmy had taken the far end of the sofa from where he normally sat, like she did, and curled those forever legs up under her like the cat Greyson had never had. She patted the sofa beside her and smiled.

"I'll just have some of yours," she purred.

Deep inside, watching as if through a porthole in the side of a starship, Ethen registered as he approached the dangerous woman that the two of them had had numerous sexual encounters on that sofa. And the chair next to it. And the counter in the kitchen area of the floorplan. And the Murphy bed that could flip up into the innermost wall to save space.

In fact, almost every horizontal surface in this apartment, including on the fire escape outside in the same rain as was falling now. The fire escape that a supposed second woman had just used to flee.

He watched appalled as Greyson Leigh moved easily within range of this sexual predator and took a seat. She reached out and took the glass from his hand, stealing the merest sip before handing it back.

Predator. Was this what it was like for his prey, looking into her eyes? He worked to keep his own fear from interfering with Greyson. Stepped fully back and trusted the man's mind to save them.

"You look like hell," she announced.

Greyson took a larger drink and swallowed caramel smoke into his stomach. Synth whiskey might not be the real stuff, but you could get it flavored just to your taste if you weren't picky. And it was still cheaper than being a purist.

He reached a hand over and brought the radio down to a whisper of what it had been.

"Ran into Zielinski today," he announced. "Or rather, he came looking for me at the noodle shop."

Ethen, looking out, noted a predatory stillness come over the woman. Correct, she had as good an opinion of the Detective/Captain as Greyson did. As Ethen did.

She watched while Greyson talked.

"They've got a bad case on their hands," he said calmly, almost introspectively, as was Greyson's style.

Calm waters run deep, as the saying goes. Ethen had not understood just how deep they could truly go before he killed Greyson Leigh and tried to control the man. Never had a victim put up such a mental struggle, nor been so fully realized in Ethen's psyche when activated.

Hopefully, that Greyson was so present now would help him dissuade Emmy from learning so much that he had to kill her. If he even could.

Still, she watched them, as if understanding that Greyson Leigh moved with a deliberate pace that would not be hurried by external forces. It was what made him such a good cop.

It was why they had taken the risk to absorb the man, before Greyson came after them next. Ethen knew now that they could not have escaped Greyson Leigh.

"They say they've got a Phrenic loose," Greyson continued. "Serial killer style, somewhere in the East. Zielinski offered me my old job to come back and stop it."

"How stupid are they?" she asked insightfully. "They asked you to come back? Just like that?"

Ethen decided to take another risk and step entirely back from Greyson's immediate presence to dive deep into the man's memories of Emmy Antúnez, letting things go like a highly-sophisticated autopilot while he was gone. Greyson could handle things better without interruption.

Successful businesswoman on her eighth start-up. Four had gone public or been bought outright by major industrial players. Personal wealth in the second thousand of humans alive, edging towards possibly joining the top group if this latest venture worked.

Unwilling to settle, she had never married. Unwilling to pursue children, she had had a medical procedure that eliminated the chance of impregnation. A wild, passionate woman who would normally mix with the steadfast, quiet Greyson Leigh like oil and water, chaos unleashed before then settling after a time.

Perhaps she needed the time of mixing as much as Greyson seemed to, and then they went back to their own lives and separated cleanly.

Oil and water.

Human social interactions still made almost no sense to Ethen.

He surfaced back into Greyson's eyes as the man took another drink and contemplated *human stupidity.*

"Enough to give me back my badge if I wanted it," he said with a hint of a shrug. "But it'll cost them."

"Good," she smiled. "That's the Greyson I know. What did you demand?"

"Zielinski retires to Florida, or back to Chicago, and the Commissioner appoints someone else in his place," Greyson took the last drink of his synth whiskey and contemplated the glass.

Normally, he only allowed himself one glass. A lesson from Epicurus on the ideal of moderation in all things. But Emmy was here. She would have needs. Greyson looked within himself and decided he had needs as well.

It had been a disrupting, uncomfortable week, like he was almost someone else at times, before he snapped back to himself randomly.

Olek Zielinski sniffing around didn't help.

"Will they go for it?" she asked as he rose and made his way to the kitchen and the bottle.

He would need to take the thing in and get it refilled soon. He had about two glasses left in this liter. Greyson shrugged to himself and poured.

"I win, either way," he turned back and studied Emmy, a perfection so pure that Michelangelo would have wept at the inadequacy of mere paint to capture her. "I go back to being a Hunter, but without that asshole Zielinski and all his little corruptions stinking up the place. Or they leave me alone and I find something else to do with my life."

She rose, unfolding like a flower turning to face the dawn. Approaching, Ethen knew a moment of pure panic at the look of carnality in her eyes, but Greyson took it in stride.

Emmy had a smell. It engulfed him as she pressed herself against his hip, one breast on either side of his ribs as her arms went around his waist. Greyson's eyes confirmed that she didn't appear to be wearing any foundation garments under her soft, canary yellow dress.

She had kicked off her heels, so she didn't look him in the eyes now. Greyson leaned down as she looked up and kissed him.

For a woman of such passions, it was tender. Calming. Yeah, she understood what today had meant for him.

Emmy broke the kiss and leaned back without breaking contact. Greyson took another sip of his synth whiskey and leaned his butt against the counter more fully, just in case she decided to climb him like a squirrel in her favorite tree.

"So what do you want from the rest of your life?" she asked simply.

As if she did anything *simple*.

His other hand went around her back, caressing her through the thin material so soft and fine she might have been nude under his touch.

"Spent the last couple of hours since Zielinski asking myself that question," Greyson finally admitted to himself. "As recently as six months ago, I would have come back without making any demands. But now?"

"Now it has been a year," she purred. "More than a year of you idling through your life, Greyson Leigh. Drinking your whiskey, listening to your music, eating your noodles. Occasionally dealing with a nymphomaniac making excessive physical demands on you. What do you want?"

Greyson smiled, and Ethen took a moment to inspect the man's memories.

Emmy was not a clinical nymphomaniac, as he understood the translation of the human term. Still, the woman had needs, and only Greyson had apparently ever been able to meet them more than once. Even more frightening.

What have I done?

He glanced once at the window to the fire escape where an imaginary other woman had fled. It was closed, so the demonic screams of passion when the woman encountered her third or fifth orgasm would probably be contained to only the floors above and below. Assuming her purpose tonight.

Greyson knew her purpose in being here, and he was a greater expert on human women than Ethen could ever imagine being.

"I'm good at puzzles," Greyson leaned down and kissed her again lightly. "Patiently unraveling a mystery until I get to the prize at the center of the maze, having slipped by the minotaur who slays so many others."

She grinned, licking her lips, and Ethen could see many other previous sexual encounters in there. Prize and minotaur suddenly made allegorical sense in a way that almost made him shiver.

Had he made a mistake, becoming Greyson Leigh?

No. Zielinski would have still found the man. Had found him. Would eventually succeed in bringing him in from the cold, to use Greyson's terminology. Would have turned the greatest Hunter in the Bureau's history loose to track a pair of stupid Phrenic who had ignored all the warnings from others and decided they were too smart for mere humans to catch them.

Greyson Leigh still frightened Ethen almost to death, even after he had become the man.

"I had arrived with grand intentions to fuck you to death," Emmy announced quietly. Tenderly. "Like usual. Maybe we should snuggle on the couch first, though."

He nodded and shifted his weight. They did not lose physical contact until she pushed him down onto his end of the sofa, then climbed into their lap like a human pet cat might.

"You'd hate business," she said more or less into his neck as she leaned herself into him, rubbing her scent all over them. "Too bureaucratic and stuffy for you."

Greyson had an arm around her, and a highball glass that might spill, but he wasn't worried. Was not the first time they had sat like this.

He had to agree with her, though. In the army, he had hated every time he had been forced to sit behind a desk with a pen, rather than climbing along balconies with a pistol or a knife. Too passive.

Too much waiting for life to happen.

Too much of what he had just spent the last year or more doing. Waiting.

"I'm just afraid they'll call my bluff," Greyson said into the frizz of brown hair on her head, seeing the first hints of grays starting to emerge like spring daffodils. "Decide they really can't do it without me."

"Can't Dominguez handle it?" she asked, leaning back enough to study his face. *Their* face. *Their* scent. *Their* being.

Ethen had never allowed a victim to remain this close to the surface before. It had never been necessary. But Zaborra had ordered it and left Ethen walking the thinnest tightrope he could imagine right now, in a ragged, gusting crosswind that would dump his silly ass into the river, where hungry sharks were circling even now.

One slip and he might not have time to take a new victim. To become somebody else.

The Hunters would have him. Would eat him, like he was supposed to do to others.

"The creature apparently killed Dominguez a week or so ago," he heard Greyson say, as if he wasn't Greyson. Wasn't in charge here. Wasn't the Phrenic who had killed a mere human and taken his form, memories, and soul.

If Greyson Leigh could have been considered a *mere* anything.

"So they need you," Emmy said conclusively. "You were the best, you know."

"I keep telling myself that," he begrudged. "You seem to keep coming back for more, in spite of other girlfriends I have to send down the fire escape when you get here."

"Pretty sure you could keep up with two of us," she purred, leaning in again and kissing him on the neck in a way that made Ethen's toes curl slightly. "Maybe even at once."

Greyson laughed in response. It wasn't the semi-hysterical

laughter that had gripped him at Zielinski's threats before. It was Greyson being Greyson.

Hunter, in more ways than one.

"We could always take a vacation," she offered, looking at him earnestly.

"We've done that," he grinned knowingly. "About a week in, we're both so stir crazy for the juice that we have to come back to the city and plunge into the madness again."

"You've had a lot of time off," Emmy noted.

"And it's the longest time I've had to sit and think in thirty years," he replied.

They replied. The lines separating Ethen and Greyson were getting blurry.

"And what have you discovered?" Emmy asked.

"That I don't have to be a killer," Greyson decided. "I'm exceptional at it. It is a job, but I don't take any joy in the doing of the thing. If it was unnecessary, I could skip it and fish, or something."

"But it is necessary?"

"Absolutely," Greyson turned his head to look her in those beautiful eyes. "We are completely insane, as a species. The aliens just held up a mirror to show how bad we were. But they also believe we can be redeemed. Even the Phrenic, as big of pains in the asses as they can be, aren't all bad. But there are always bad people out there, and sometimes you gotta have a person with a gun standing in the way."

"My hero," she breathed into the skin of his neck.

Ethen listened to the man he was impersonating. Found the memories behind the words.

It was becoming a struggle, keeping them separated into two parts. And it would get worse long before it ever got better, as he might have to maintain this person for six months, rather than the week or three normally required for a heist or assassination.

He was walking into the lion's den, to use Greyson's vocabulary. Lying down with the lions themselves and hoping he could somehow escape in the morning.

For a moment, Ethen felt a surge of pure rage pass through him like a gravity wave.

Zaborra had assigned him the role of killing the cop and impersonating the human for a long stretch. Ethen's partner could continue bouncing between his victims, killing as he needed to, while never having to live with someone like Greyson Leigh in his soul.

Never face that man in the mirror.

"Hey," the human woman suddenly grabbed his chin and forced it around to look at her. "Whatever it is, it's not that bad. You're Greyson Leigh, the most stubborn, dangerous man I've ever met. Whatever those shits at the Bureau think, they need you to save their asses, not the other way around. Okay?"

She was talking to the human whose face he wore, but Ethen took heart in her words, as if she could see inside him to what evil lurked in the man's soul. Other evil, besides being the shell of a slightly-panicked shapeshifter wondering how far he was in over his head.

He could be Greyson Leigh. He could be a Hunter. A killer many considered the most dangerous man ever in the Bureau. Looking around, Greyson had a better life than Ethen had ever lived, drab and quiet as it might be.

Maybe there was indeed something to this role that he could live with. Zaborra might throw a fit later, but Ethen had the perfect cover, especially if the authorities didn't realize that two Phrenic had landed, and thought they only had one.

Maybe he should go all in, pretending to be Greyson Leigh, and hunt down the infamous Zaborra Strani and take him down.

He could hide inside Greyson Leigh's life, at least for a while. It was a far better place than anything he had ever done for himself.

Ethen let go of the anger that had wanted to take root and smiled crookedly down at the woman curled up in his lap.

There would be other fringe benefits, as well.

[3]

MORNING

It was a dream of being swallowed by a huge snake, after it had chased him through an impossible jungle Greyson couldn't remember ever visiting. The jolt sat him upright in his bed, convinced he was on the wrong planet, in the wrong life, and there was no clue pointing him back to sanity.

Even the gravity felt wrong.

He slid from bed and pulled on pants to go with the underwear and shirt he had put back on when Emmy had left. He couldn't sleep without a shirt on, even if he did without a blanket on the hot nights of August.

Like a career bachelor, he made up the Murphy bed and lofted it back into the wall so he could have the fold-out table underneath. Sun was just starting to glow through the single layer of cloth he used as a curtain, so he set about to making some coffee, knowing sleep would be a waste of time now.

In the old fashioned gangster movies his dad used to watch when Greyson was a kid, the private detective hero would have a smoke right about now, maybe rolling it himself from pipe tobacco. Nobody smoked anymore, but he supposed he could have taken up one of the other habits that had replaced it, if he was an addictive personality.

Music and whiskey were enough. But coffee was going to be necessary. He had a bad feeling about the day.

Grabbing his handheld, he checked messages. Discreet commentary from Emmy that meant she would sleep well with an animated kiss emoji. The usual junk that companies paid to get around the filters. One from Olek Jan Zielinski.

"You better be fucking worth it, punk," was all it read.

That was all it needed to.

Greyson grinned as he ladled the grounds into the machine and added water. Ethen sat right behind the man and watched over a shoulder, like a parrot, if he understood the obscure reference.

He would have to continue to be Greyson Leigh, in thought as well as deed. Instantiate the cop, rather than merely impersonate him, like he might do with a simple bank manager. Go so deep into the role that they risked becoming permanently inseparable.

Ethen wondered if he would ever want to come out again.

He was Phrenic. They stole other people's lives by killing them. This was the first time Ethen had ever imagined keeping one afterwards, instead of just dropping it in a trashcan on his way out of town. Keeping this small studio on the seventh floor. Living a careful, frugal life with synth whiskey, udon, and classical music. Survive the insane sexual demands of Emmy with Greyson Leigh's categorical aplomb.

Hide inside the Hunter Bureau, next to the very people that wanted to kill him.

Hide inside Greyson Leigh.

Because Greyson was a better man than he was. Holding

the cop up next to Zaborra just made that much obvious. He didn't even dare put himself in that image to compare.

Ethen walked to a chester and pulled open the drawer at knee level, rooting around until he found the Guild Communicator hidden there in a pile of undershirts. The parts went together and the machine powered itself up with a low beep as the coffee brewed and they walked over to dig some coconut milk out of the fridge.

He didn't dare leave it assembled for long. Someone might notice the signal and track it here eventually, but for a few minutes, he could pretend that he had been born on another planet, far away from these dangerous monkeys. And that he might be planning to go back again someday. That he might not was a thing Ethen didn't even dare whisper to himself yet.

Contact made. Infiltration probable.

He clicked send and pulled the power supply back out, as well as the mothercard, resting the three pieces on the counter as he poured.

Let Zaborra make of that what he will. It had been his plan, once they realized that their cover as Dyarnan tourists had been blown. Ethen would become the one cop even Dominguez had feared, from the few memories Ethen had tasted before the human's partner had shot him.

Palmstunner, dead center mass. Like the woman had been trained to. Drop anybody, including most alien species.

Most.

Phrenic had a secondary nervous system that humans and G'schtack and the rest lacked. Ethen had rerouted everything and fled, but in that tiny taste he had learned about another cop. A better cop. A hunter even a terrible man like Dominguez feared, sitting right at the top of the man's mind.

Greyson Leigh.

And so Zaborra had ordered him to kill the man. Ethen hadn't argued, just slipped into his apartment when he was asleep. Pounced on the man's dreams and ate his mind.

Zaborra hadn't been here. Hadn't watched the mind of Greyson Leigh fight back, refuse to fracture under the stress like all the others ever had. It hadn't helped Ethen that he needed to remain in this guise twenty-four/seven until they knew how the police would react. Had to live with Greyson front and center, until they started to bleed together.

My God, what would he be like in six months, if he kept this up? Would he even remember how to be Ethen Boli? Or would he have fallen down the well of Greyson Leigh's mind so far that he drowned?

Worse, would he mind becoming the other man?

They added a dash of milk to the coffee and stirred it, already unsure where one piece of them left off and the other began.

It was only going to get worse, wasn't it?

[4]

RACHEL

GREYSON HAD FINISHED THE SMALL POT OF COFFEE, really just two big mugs worth, and gotten through most of the news boards. The device he was using wasn't as sophisticated as a Guild Communicator, but they were distant cousins, like the Guild itself considered the primitives of this planet. Yokels, many of the aliens would have said, meeting city folk for the first time in depth.

He sighed as the machine chirped with an incoming message. The sun was up and he had opened both the curtain and the window. Wasn't sitting on the fire escape because of the threat of drizzle, but Emmy wanting to leave her scent on it last night still played in his mind. They hadn't, but that wasn't the same as wouldn't.

The message was from Rachel Asher. Patrolman/Hunter. Dominguez's former partner and the one that had apparently driven off the Phrenic when it killed the man.

Good thing she only had a palmstunner, Ethen whispered in the darkness.

Greyson grunted noncommittally and put his empty

mug in the sink after running water in it. The tower water was clean these days, but that was an alien device installed at the base of the stack that did some mumbo-jumbo to filter it.

He didn't mind, but it had been a chore, learning to drink coffee all over again once the water didn't have any residual taste to it.

Inbound to pick you up, the message from Asher read. *Don't figure you're asleep.*

He hadn't worked with the kid all that much before. She had only been a Hunter for about two years now, and he'd been gone for more than one of them. Still, Zielinski had partnered her with Dominguez, his boy, so she must be pretty good.

Young to be a Hunter, but the force wanted skills as much as experience. Being a stone killer was still more important than having a network of stooges and contacts. You could build or inherit the latter.

It was like the old basketball saying: You can't teach tall.

Greyson assumed she would be the minder assigned to hold his hand. The one that would learn his skills and keep them fresh for the next generation.

Jesus. Stop it, you aren't that old.

Didn't help that Rachel Asher was young enough to be his daughter. And old enough to be a multi-year veteran of Metroplex Police before she got accepted into Earth Police Special Missions on the basis of her test scores.

You're just feeling old today, Greyson. What do you want to be when you grow up?

A cop, but he wasn't sure he still had it in him. Too much stress, the last month or so. And this last week had just been the kind of hell where some mornings he woke up on the wrong planet, and others he came awake fighting mad.

He changed into comfortable slacks and a nice-enough shirt. Greyson had ceremonially burned all his ties after he got fired, so he couldn't put one on now without waiting for a haberdashery to open, and he really didn't care. They got him like this and liked it, or they could go piss up a rope.

The shoes were on their third resoling, but they had been his one indulgence when he got this job. Semi-armored tops. Spike-proof bottoms. Low profile and waterproof and warm. It still snowed in Boston in the winter.

He grabbed his chocolate-brown longcoat, the one that had enough Kevlar to stop old-fashioned bullets and tangle up knives, down from the peg just inside the door and turned left instead of right as he exited his flat, taking the stairs down instead of the elevator. Kept a man in shape to go up and down stairs all the time.

Hunters don't cut corners. Especially not with Phrenic serial killers on the loose.

The only thing that was missing was a gun and a badge, but Greyson expected that to change shortly.

Did it make him happy?

He shrugged as he emerged in the lobby. He wasn't dead. The bad guys hadn't all retired to Florida or off-world colonies.

He had a life, and if they were going to walk into it again, he would adjust. He did that.

Adjust.

World could go to hell, and Greyson Leigh would just nod, put his head down, and push on through.

Made him what he was.

Greyson looked around as he emerged onto a sidewalk so old it had cracks in it. Honest to God concrete, and not the new stuff prettier neighborhoods were redoing everything with.

No patrol cars evident, but that didn't mean anything.

A hand emerge from a car window. Not waving, just up

once and down. Pulled back inside once Asher was sure he had seen her.

Humans are designed to track on motion first and color second. Hunters have that drilled into them relentlessly, because frequently an alien moves wrong. They don't have the same programming or center of gravity that a human does.

You sit in a sidewalk café and work to identify every species of creature that walks by, including their native gravity field, so that one of the strangers can't hide as a human. At least not for long.

Phrenic were different. They became humans in all the ways that mattered, when they wanted to. But they still had tells. Little unconscious things that gave them away, at least to someone paying real close attention.

Somewhere, Ethen Boli nodded, keeping his hands off the controls and letting this thing called Greyson Leigh operate as if this was his body they were in, rather than a shell that looked like him. Smelled like him.

Tasted like him, if Emelina Antúnez had been fooled last night.

Greyson nodded and jaywalked, once he was sure no dumb-ass Texan driving a taxi was going to run him over. They had auto-driving vehicles these days, but with so many people out of work from the militaries being downsized, automation had kind of taken a generation or two off. There was enough money floating around that everyone could make a decent living, but lots of people needed something to do to give them purpose, and not everyone could paint.

Coast clear, he crossed behind the grayish sedan that looked like a simple ground car. Chandler didn't make these, but allowed the government to rebadge the things so that from any distance they looked like a late model Chandler Jouster.

At least until you started flying. Jouster didn't have that option.

Locks popped as he approached, so Greyson pulled the door open and slid in. Windows didn't look one-way from the outside, but that was an old cop trick, too. Just looked grimy, which you got in this town when a hot, gritty summer faded into the wet season. Like now.

Nobody was in back, though. Or they were ducked down in the foot well like assassins. Greyson didn't figure he was that important, so he closed the door and let the various safety systems harness him in without bitching.

Seatbelts didn't work all that well if you were falling out of the sky, so Guild Skycruisers had all sorts of other things built in, but it still had to pass DMV regulations, so they included seat belts, too.

"Long time, no see, old man," Rachel turned a cool gaze on him as she rolled her window up and put the machine in gear.

Or whatever you did with Guild technology masquerading as something humans built.

Greyson and Ethen could appreciate that fine edge of weirdness.

Greyson studied the youngster. Latina, like Emmy, but darker. Mestizo, to use the old distinction, rather than Indian, but even more American than him, since her great-great-great-something grandparents had been born in California before the *blancos* ever came long and called it a state.

Most Americans were mutts of some sort. Racism like Zielinski indulged in was just a way of hating anybody a different shade or religion. Stupid, but nobody had made Greyson God long enough to fix it.

"Still taking classes?" Greyson asked.

Every quarter, something else. Every meal it seemed like

the woman had shoveled food into her mouth quickly so she had time to read some textbook.

"Uh huh," she nodded, pulling out into the non-existence traffic.

Nobody but cops and delivery drivers were out at six in the morning.

"How soon?" Greyson asked, wondering if the woman's aggressive schedule had changed.

"Two more years," Rachel turned just enough to grin at him as she drove.

The hardass who had been sitting in the driver's seat when he got into the vehicle vanished for just a moment.

"After that, Scotland Yard, here I come," she continued with a girlish smile. "Kiss all you losers on the mouth and off to the big time."

They both knew that England had stopped being a world power a long time ago, but there was something about the old Metropolitan Police Service, serving most of the London Metroplex, that called to some cops. Rachel Asher included.

Too many old BBC shows, Greyson guessed. The romance and glory wasn't going to be any different there than it was here, but it was London, and that was probably exotic enough for Rachel.

She wouldn't necessarily stand out like a sore thumb these days, given the wide collection of ethnicities that came from the old colonies, but she would probably be the only Latina in the department.

Greyson grunted and nodded approvingly at the youngster's dreams. He'd never bothered with college, enlisting when he was seventeen and becoming a killer instead. Rachel Asher was taking night courses in accounting and law, just because she wanted to end up a Big Shot with a London office corner view when she was his age.

"You haven't asked where we're going," Rachel pointed

out after a few minutes, as the hum of the tires mesmerized him.

"Unless Zielinski is about to pop out of the back seat with a gun or a bottle, I assume someplace where important people will make empty speeches about reconciliation and new futures. Maybe a few snapshots for the rags. A couple of quiet threats whispered in the men's room not to mess with certain swindles or politicians. And then to work hunting."

Greyson turned his head to watch the impact of the words on the young cop.

Her face went blank.

"Put a shilling on it?" he grinned.

"No bet, old man," Rachel laughed. "I forget you used to be pretty good at this sort of thing."

Greyson lapsed into silence and watched the sun climb the skies. They were headed to the old downtown, the quiet buildings not that far from the ancient port that had once been the point of entry for a bunch of radicals intent on stealing an entire continent from the folks that had lived here first. Before Ellis Island.

Cars started to join them on the road. Not many, but those folks who needed to get to the office early, maybe for meetings with folks in Moscow or Paris. Earth never slept, regardless of the folks living here.

Greyson leaned his head back and fought off a headache with closed eyes and careful breathing.

"You need to stop and get food, Leigh?" Asher's voice intruded. "Coffee? Anything?"

"Had coffee," he said simply. "Depending on them, I expect you and I will have an early lunch today. Just my head, looking forward to dealing with all the old gang."

She grunted in turn and fell into a companionable silence, the hum of tires a monotonous drone in the background like a phone that had somehow never disconnected from a call.

The lion's den was coming. Ethen Boli was going to have to pretend to be a cop, even as he and Greyson Leigh pretended to be lions.

[5]

COMMISSIONER

Greyson really didn't come back to life until Rachel had parked the car in a secured garage underground, the kind with garage doors that would require anti-tank missiles to penetrate, before she led him to the elevator bank.

It all came flooding back to him at that point.

The years he had spent in this exact spot, waiting for too few elevators to serve too big of a building. There were stairs, but they were locked from the other side, forcing you to use the elevators going up.

If you wanted in, you were getting scanned, sniffed, and identified by one of those smart systems that had everyone's image on file.

So he waited, more alive now than he had been all morning, it seemed, the past being just a thin fog that never quite obscured the distance, and never quite revealed it.

Greyson figured he was getting old, and philosophical.

Mean would come later.

Finally the doors opened and admitted him and Rachel into the holy ground of law enforcement. At least until Scotland Yard accepted her.

The elevator closed and all the scanners came on. Greyson felt a twitch he couldn't explain run through his soul, but the lift started to move and he felt himself relaxing. He could feel Rachel's eyes on him, but he just let go a deep sigh, leaned his head back, and looked to the heavens for inspiration.

Sixth floor. Not fourth where all the working stiffs lived. Six, where the important people had their own cafeteria separate from the beat cops downstairs.

The doors opened onto a sparse reception area. Couple of couches and a few chairs, if you were early for a meeting, or they just wanted you to cool your jets and be reminded how unimportant you were, compared to them.

Greyson didn't recognize the young redhead behind the desk, but they had never seemed to last long. Either they were good and got moved to better things further back, or they weren't and the hiring agency sent someone else tomorrow.

Didn't matter. There was someone he did recognize, standing discreetly off to one side.

Edgar Redhawk. Tribal Sioux from some band in the Dakotas. Greyson had never looked too closely. Hadn't mattered. Similarly, the man was forty-something, and that was as much detail as he ever let on to, only relevant because he understood some of the old jokes that kids like Rachel wouldn't get.

They locked eyes and Greyson got a feel for the amount of angry politics that must have been swept off the table by raging words, for the two of them to be standing here this morning.

It wasn't personal.

As far as Greyson knew, Redhawk didn't do personal. Everything was business with him, including political assassinations.

Greyson nodded and stepped closer. Redhawk was also the Executive Assistant to local Police Commissioner Buford Owens. Chief of the man's staff, right hand. Assassin, if necessary. They'd been paying attention to the scanners, and when the system announced Greyson Leigh was in the building, Redhawk had emerged.

No small talk. Just a quick look up and down, scowling slightly at the lack of a tie, and then a sharp nod.

"This way," Redhawk said, turning and using the card on a lanyard to key the door open.

Greyson followed, with Rachel right on his heels. Today would probably be an education for her, since he doubted she'd ever been sucked into a shitshow like this one promised to be.

In through a maze of desks and head-high barriers, towards the offices on the west wall, where there had once been a view of the river, when buildings and egos around here were smaller.

The door was closed when they approached, itself surrounded by a large, open space with comfortable chairs and a coffee robot that had ten thousand settings you could program.

Greyson wondered if they had erased him from that system, too.

Redhawk knocked at the door, waited a beat, and opened it in just enough to stick his head into the space while Greyson and Rachel got watched by others who just happened to find some excuse to be milling about or meandering.

Circus tiger, that's me, Greyson kept his body language petite and gray.

Redhawk opened the door the rest of the way and gestured for Greyson to enter.

"Asher, you wait here for now," he said simply, gesturing towards the chairs.

Rachel had read the room correctly. She already had her handheld out and was reading homework by the time Greyson followed the other man into the office.

The door closed and Greyson couldn't help but think of the old fashioned gas chamber that states like California had used in a more primitive era.

He had been expecting Commissioner Owens. He hadn't been expecting the man to have been evicted from his own desk, standing next his ego wall—the one with all the pictures of him meeting famous people—while trying to look natural. And failing.

And even then, it was odd seeing a man nearly seven feet tall, three hundred pounds, sheathed in a bespoke silk suit, looking like he had wandered into the wrong office by mistake.

Behind the desk, given Owens being over here, Greyson had been expecting the Head Police Commissioner, Yulia Kwan, up from Columbia. But she had given way as well, and was seated primly in one of the two chairs on this side of that vast expanse of hand-polished cherry oak.

Kwan was a Vladivostok Russian/Hong Kong mix, ethnically, that had always reminded Greyson of the actress Michelle Yeoh, from the early part of the century. Almost as pretty, quite a bit taller. Just as deadly as many of that actress's roles.

The left the woman behind the desk.

Her Honor Denise Upkins, *Metropolitan* of the entire Eastern Metroplex itself, seated behind Owens's desk. Must have flown up from Gotham last night, or maybe she was the one that had sicced Zielinski on him in the first place yesterday.

She was a tall black woman from Maryland originally.

Early fifties, so just a little above his age, without cutting it too fine. Old school pol who hadn't been able to break into the political machine that had once been Tammany Hall, so she had built her own machine instead, and broken those silly bastards who used to think they owned Gracie Mansion.

She was probably the most dangerous of the three of them. Maybe all four, including him, depending on how you wanted to slice that cake. Redhawk didn't count, except as his would be the fingerprints on the execution orders one of the others signed.

"Sit, Leigh," *Her Honor* ordered, pointing at the empty chair.

He did, noting that Edgar had taken up his usual space to *Her Honor*'s right, as if Owens was sitting there instead.

Idly, Greyson wondered if Owens was in the process of being fired, and they just hadn't told him or anyone else yet. Lots of churn going on, if Greyson Leigh was back in the building.

She studied him back, eyes lingering on the center of his chest.

"You aren't wearing a tie, Leigh," she said abruptly.

"I don't own a tie," he fired back with a bit of a feral grin, feeling his oats just a little this morning.

There was a pause while she processed that tidbit.

"Zielinski talked to you yesterday," she finally announced, as if anybody here was ignorant of the fact.

"That's right," Greyson acknowledged, still wondering what one of the off-world colonies might make of an ex-soldier, ex-cop, presumably-reformed killer looking for a new start.

"You made unreasonable demands, for a man who is unemployed and has been for more than a year," she noted, fixing him with those deadly brown eyes of hers.

"Define unreasonable," Greyson replied slowly,

enunciating every syllable with his own edge, turning to scowl angrily up at Commissioner Owens, lurking close by. "A year ago, there might have been a really good case to be made about corrupt dealings around here, sub-rosa with members of the Illymus Merchant Guild."

Greyson waited for the giant man to flinch before he turned back to *Her Honor*.

"Investigating such allegations may have been one of the reasons I was removed from employment, *Your Honor*," he said in a tight, angry voice. "You'll have to ask the men in charge of the case after I left how all that worked out afterwards."

Good to know he hadn't lost all his emotional depth, with the recent, unexplained turmoil. Or his way with words.

"I've had cause to review your last few cases, Leigh," Upkins said in a matronly tone, like the old woman at Church who would strip your hide with her tongue if you got out of line. "Several of them, in fact, because I wanted to see if others were correct that you might be the best cop for the situation."

Greyson just watched her. She hadn't asked a question. He didn't feel like volunteering anything else.

She seemed to appreciate that.

"There have been whispers of previous improprieties," *Her Honor* continued in a lower tone. Conspiratorial. Angry, even. "Detective/Captain Zielinski's name came up more than once, although no concrete evidence was ever presented before a grand jury."

No, there wouldn't have been, would there? Too much risk of too many people being taken down, if someone turned the lights on and watched all the cockroaches madly scamper for the corners.

Greyson missed the good old days of his childhood, before so much of the press in this country had been neutered by laws and economics. The muckraking days. People didn't care anymore, as long as the power stayed on, food was cheap, and entertainment vids could fill the empty places where they might have once had lives.

"In the interest of resolving matters around this case, Captain Zielinski has chosen to take retirement, as a way to clear the decks around here," *Her Honor* said knowingly. "A fresh start, as it were."

Greyson assumed that they had offered him retirement at current pay, plus keeping his racist mouth shut. That, or be facing a grand jury indictment that would require him to name names as a way to keep his sentence anything less than *forever*.

Or ninjas.

Olek Zielinski was the kind of rat bastard who probably would have burned everything down, just to make sure nobody else got away either, if he had to take a fall.

No wonder Owens was so nervous. And Chief Commissioner Kwan probably wasn't resting easily on her throne today either. Not if *Her Honor* was taking a personal interest in things.

Greyson smiled. Not even reinstated, and he had already made the world a better place.

What could he do with a badge and a gun?

"Fresh start," Greyson echoed the woman, adding the appropriate nod she had apparently been expecting before she continued.

"We're not sure who the new captain of the Hunter Bureau in this district will be," *Her Honor* continued. "I'm given to understand you just might walk right back out the door if I offered it to you."

"That would be correct, Metropolitan Upkins," Greyson said. "Politics and paperwork are the two things I hate most in this life."

"Would you stay around?" she asked.

He presumed she meant after he caught the rogue Phrenic, *freak* as most of the cops around here would call the creature.

Greyson shrugged loosely inside his big longcoat. Expansively, even.

"Depends on the situation around the building, I'd guess," he offered. "Did fine when I was a cop. Did fine when I wasn't."

He left it at that. The three people in the room with him, not counting Redhawk, were possibly the most powerful, dangerous politicians north of Cape Fear and east of the Mississippi River.

Greyson really didn't care what they did in the privacy of their own homes, as long as their little swindles didn't hurt other people who couldn't protect themselves with a badge. Every cop has a limit. His was just shorter than most of the others.

Her Honor seemed to appreciate that about him.

He still had no idea why she was involved in this. Easier to issue orders, so you had a fall guy. Unless your Chief Commissioner refused, and you had to do things yourself. That was the only play that made any sense.

Sweep the entire Police Commission clear and start over? Must be one hell of a something, back there in the shadows thrown by a rogue Phrenic killer.

Greyson wasn't sure if he wanted to look or not. Maybe he'd sic Asher on it, tomorrow. Give the kid something to do to make her look good for the London folks. After all, getting your political superiors arrested for graft and corruption would certainly make a splash, as long as it didn't make you completely unemployable tomorrow.

"Will you come back to duty, Leigh?" Upkins asked in a simple, honest tone. "Be reinstated? Pretend that none of this happened and you've just been assigned the next hunt?"

He could make that promise.

Didn't cover Asher, so if she went off and did things?

Hey, kid's ambitious. How'm I supposed to stop her?

"As long as I don't have Zielinski breathing over my shoulder," Greyson acknowledged, before he turned back to Owens with a hard face. "Or others who might not understand how many cooks the kitchen can hold comfortably."

He turned back to Metropolitan Upkins just fast enough to catch a ghost of a grin on her face. Like Greyson Leigh was going to be doing her other favors as he took down a serial killer. Maybe setting up all of her Police Commission to take a fall, too?

"Edgar, you will prepare the necessary paperwork and backdate it so Leigh continued to accrue seniority and union membership benefits from that unfortunate date," she glanced back at her lethal shadow and got a nod. "Buford, you will sign it. Am I clear?"

"You are," Commissioner Owens said, the first sound he had made since Greyson had walked in, other than silk swishing as he moved.

"Good, all of you out now," she ordered. "I wish to talk to Detective/Hunter Leigh privately."

At least as privately as this office might manage, given the number of recording and transmitting devices Greyson expected were within range.

So his jaw nearly hit the carpet, after they were alone and the door closed, when she pulled a…*device* from the pocket of her blazer and set it on the desk between them. She pushed a button on the top and Greyson heard barks of squelch and saw motes of smoke appear in a few places around the walls.

She smiled like a cat with the best cream. Greyson didn't find it comforting. She probably knew that.

"Do you know what a stalking horse is, Leigh?" *Her Honor* asked with that same smile.

"Target you use when hunting big cats," he answered. "Stake it to the ground out there to get killed, figuring you can shoot the killer when it comes. Nobody ever worries too much about the horse."

"I'm not that worried about you, Greyson," she nodded. "They said you were still the best, so I went and got you. And I'm tying you to a stake for some big kitty cats to stalk. There's probably not much I can do to protect you from them, other than avenge you later, but I also wouldn't mind if that horse kicked a few times before he went down. Clear?"

Greyson smiled at her.

"Asher my partner?" he asked.

"She is," *Her Honor* smiled back, warmer this time. "Another stone killer like you, who also happens to be a good cop."

"Kill them all, and make God sort them out?" Greyson cocked his head at the woman.

"If I'm the only survivor, I get to write the after-action reports, soldier."

[6]

LUNCH

Greyson had directed Rachel to a spot down on the old South Side. The neighborhood had been ugly, gentrified, fallen down again, and was fighting another round of gentrification tooth and nail, but it would lose this one as well.

Money was more important than culture. Especially the old traces of Southie nobody but the grumpy old locals wanted to preserve.

Tommy had opened his burger joint not long before the Guild had broken the sky open. He still served the best fries Greyson had ever found in his years with a gun. The burgers weren't all that bad, either.

Since he might have back pay coming, Greyson splurged and got a double order of french fries today, home cut and fried in peanut oil and Tommy's special seasoning mix. Rachel had finished hers and was sneaking the odd one off his plate, probably unconsciously.

"She really said that?" the young woman was aghast.

Whether it was the Metropolitan admitting those things,

or just the weirdness of the situation wasn't all that clear, but Greyson didn't have much better of an idea himself.

"She did," Greyson replied, taking the second-to-last bite of his burger and swishing it down with some cola.

"And you're okay with that, Greyson?" Rachel asked.

"Figured something like that was coming when Zielinski walked out of the rain yesterday to bend my ear," he grabbed some more fries and stuffed them in his mouth before she got them all. "Those folks don't play nice."

"Yeah, that's for certain," Rachel finished her drink and leaned back. "And Owens is not necessarily on our side?"

"None of them are on our side, kid," he laughed. "Just make sure they don't ruin your career when they get around to destroying mine."

"Aren't we all supposed to be on the same side here?" she leaned forward again and snagged some more of those addicting fries.

"No," Greyson countered with a harsh laugh. "We're all cops. Not even remotely the same thing. They don't want me back, and it was bad enough that both Commissioners had to have gotten overridden by Upkins. There will be bad blood later over this, but I'm pretty sure she's counting on you heading to London at some point, and me leaving when I'm ready. That lets her take all the credit, and annihilate the fools who made her get involved."

"*Jesus,*" she whistled.

"Yeah, but right now everybody has to play nice with us," Greyson said. "At least until we bring them back a body for the news to spend a couple of days frothing about."

"London won't take me without a degree, Greyson," Rachel pointed out. "That's two years from now."

"Kid, we make *Her Honor* look good on this one, and I'm pretty sure that she'll put in a personal call to the Mayor of London," Greyson said.

"That bad?"

Her eyes had probably not opened that much since she was six, but Greyson figured it was better she go through this with him, now, at the beginning, than have to do it later, when things got fast and hairy.

"She made Zielinski leave town, Rachel," Greyson said. "Owens looks to be on a very short leash, or noose, depending. I was close to taking down a lot of folks when they hauled me in and fired me. That hasn't gone away, just because they need you and me to hunt down a shapeshifting killer."

"That's the part about the horse kicking," Rachel guessed.

"That's right," he agreed.

"And you're just going to take it?" she asked.

"Oh, no, kid. We're not going to take anything from those people."

$$[\ 7 \ ]$$

BEEN THERE BEFORE

DÉJÀ VU.

Greyson looked around Dominguez's tattered apartment and seemed to see it through two or three sets of eyes, which almost made him wobbly enough to lean on the door jamb, but they managed to hold it together.

They?

Weird.

Because he worked better at night, Greyson had taken Rachel back to the office after lunch to finally pick up his new badge and be officially issued both a palmstunner and a nerve scrambler.

He didn't buy the story that his old badge had been misplaced. Zielinski had probably melted it down as a paperweight trophy. Olek was that petty. Most likely they'd find it in Florida one of these days, if anybody cared that much.

Officially a cop again, he'd spent the rest of the day reading reports while the kid did homework and fielded the odd question from the old man across the desk in the filing room filled with evidence. Wasn't much to go on, but there never were in cases like this, at least until your killer had already spent a year doing his deeds.

Hadn't been that long, or that many victims, so at sunset they headed out to the most recent crime scene. Cop on duty assured him that nobody had bothered the Police tape across the front door. Place had been sealed up from the inside well enough and at least one uniform was on twenty-four/seven for a while.

Not many cops got killed in their own apartment.

Place had been stripped to the walls, so it wasn't the dump Greyson had been expecting. He wondered if Zielinski had sent someone through ahead of time, to make sure nothing incriminating would be found in the course of innocent lab techs doing their job.

There'd been a struggle in the living room. He'd known that. All the furniture was gone now, but the Bureau had a nifty device the Guild had given them. Recreated a holographic image of the room as it had been when the techs arrived.

Greyson pulled out the projector and set it to hovering just inside the living room, next to the entry hall where the front bathroom was. He clicked a button and watched the machine turn itself on and map the space.

Rachel hadn't said a word since she entered, but he wasn't surprised. She'd be having her own flashbacks, but Greyson had been a cop long enough, so he figured walking her through it would be less traumatic now and more cathartic later.

"You were at the door?" Greyson checked back over the shoulder she barely cleared behind him.

"That's right," she replied, jaw a little tight and eyes a little wide. "Heard something just as I was about to knock. Didn't sound right, so I kicked the door in. Figured I could always apologize later if there was somebody in bondage gear hanging from the ceiling."

Greyson turned enough to really study the woman. Five foot two, in shoes, maybe. Not petite, but also not built like a colonial space marine you saw in the vids, either. She smiled up at him, as if she could read his mind, but if that were the case, she'd have already shot him, so he smiled back.

Still, either Dominguez had forgotten to set all his security, or Rachel Asher was stronger than she looked. Good to know, since she was the one that might have to save his ass later.

Greyson stood at the entryway, feet still on the cheap entry linoleum rather than the cheaper, taupe carpet, and let the machine display what Rachel had seen.

Sofa, already soiled because someone had cracked Dominguez's face open to bleed on it. Coffee table flipped with those stupid picture books scattered everywhere. The ones the man never read and just used to impress women he had conned into coming back to his place.

Lamp in the corner had stayed upright through it all, so they had good light to see a projection of Dominguez's body half on the couch and half off.

"Then what?" Greyson knelt to change his perspective on the scene and felt Rachel joining him.

Hopefully, she would learn better habits from him than she had from her former partner.

What if she figures us out? a voice echoed strangely.

Then we're freshly cooked meat, another one answered. Made no sense, but crime scenes rarely did.

"It was standing over him, tentacles licking his face or something," Rachel's voice had gotten small and tight.

Cop voice, when the brain steps back far enough that you can try not to remember the smells of dying, or hear a man's life rattle out of his lungs.

"Close enough," Greyson said. "They feed on your mental energy by tasting the chemistry of your brain with fine cilia on those tentacles. Get your memories when they get your DNA so they can morph into you later."

"Yeah," she agreed vaguely. "Ugly thing was making a sound. Had the palmstunner in my hand, so I shot it. Didn't work."

No, it hadn't, thank the ancient ones.

"Palmstunner won't hurt a Phrenic, Rachel," Greyson told her. "Well, it hurts them, but won't drop one. That's why you and I have them in ankle holsters as backup, and nerve scramblers under our arms. And you have to be at less than fifty meters to do more than just knock one down with a nerve scrambler. Outside that, they can still crawl away."

"You've hunted one?" she asked breathlessly. "Killed one?"

"Yeah," Greyson nodded. "Not too many ever try their luck on Earth, but they're one of the reasons Hunter Bureau exists, for the most part. I might be the expert, among humans at least."

And most other species, but Ethen didn't even think that thought too loud. Yes, he knew his own kind as well as any, and had added the amazing database of knowledge and experience that was Greyson Leigh to it. Frightening, really, what they might be as a combined entity.

"So it ran?" Greyson prompted.

"Did," Rachel agreed. "Damned thing bounced straight up like an armadillo, off the ceiling, then the wall by the kitchen, and back up the hallway to the bedroom. Never seen anything like it."

Greyson found the spot on the ceiling, as if it had been his own hand. Then the one on the wall that had actually been his foot pushing off. He stood and brushed his hands down the front of his pants to dry them.

Nerves.

Just to get himself deeper into cop mode, he drew the newly-issued nerve scrambler and held it barrel-up in his right hand.

When he was a kid, there had been a huge burst of science fiction cinema, as the technology of imagination got good enough and cheap enough to show anything you could want on a green screen.

Nerve scrambler looked like an old Buck Rogers ray gun from the pulp days a century earlier, rather than the darker, militaristic stuff of his youth. Gold plated, with a thin layer of real gold as a non-reactive surface. Emitter at the far end with a double cone like an old fashioned television satellite dish, one sitting inside another. Even made a Buck Rogers kind of sound when you pulled the trigger.

Not as much recoil as a palmstunner, so it took some getting used to, or you'd end up shooting your target in his balls instead of his heart. Both hurt, but the one was a really embarrassing way to die.

Rachel drew hers as well, but Greyson couldn't tell if she was mirroring him, or had gotten some of his inner nervousness. Probably both.

The little things that kept you alive as a cop. Hopefully, nobody was hiding in the bedroom, because Greyson was pretty sure his instincts would kill them before his brain processed who they were.

Another stupid way to die.

He stalked down the hallway, suddenly back in a jungle somewhere he couldn't talk about, even twenty-three years later, moving in on someone who never saw it coming.

They never had in those days.

Body sideways to minimize silhouette. Quiet feet shuffling firmly across the carpet down the left edge of the space. Left hand out to stop a knife or grab a handful of clothing. Right hand back, making it hard for someone to get at his gun.

Rachel was left-handed, so she was his exact opposite, across the hallway and back a few steps.

Mirrors.

Empty kitchen and living room were behind them. Greyson glanced into the spare bedroom that was unused from the images. He hadn't told the projector to stay put, so it was with them going down the hallway and recreating rooms for him as it did.

Greyson had lived in a two bedroom place like this once. The spare had been his library, filled with old books that he had eventually decided he could read electronically just as easily, so he had downsized to the studio and parted with almost everything except the coffee maker.

That was too important to leave to chance when you had a really good one.

Linen closet across from the spare bedroom was empty and smelled of fabric softener. Washer/dryer unit next to that in a cubbyhole.

Dominguez had always used a maid service, as far back as Greyson remembered, so presumably they stored things in here and did their work while he was out. Hopefully someone had let them know their contract had expired.

Master bedroom.

Plain walls until the projector got inside the door and lit it up with the extravagant definition of decadence by a man who didn't know what a *Lothario* was. Bed big enough for four to sleep comfortably. Doorways to the master bathroom and walk-in closet that were behind the laundry space.

Dresser for leaving stuff. Projector showed Dominguez's badge, gun, wallet, and pocket change. Handheld had been on his body when they found them.

Art on the walls was just past that edge of tasteful

pornography that folks like Olivia and Nagel had managed so well, or going back to the classics: Gil Elvgren and Antonio Vargas. This was just trashy porn meant to look high-brow. Movie posters for bad shows you might stumble onto in the hours just before dawn. Or old Italian cinema.

Art drawn by teenage boys instead of masters. The kind who were looking down on women as objects, rather than worshiping them. But that described Dominguez to a *T*.

Greyson stuck his head into the bathroom, let the projector show him the closet with all those expensive suits that a man on Dominguez's salary shouldn't have been able to afford. And the handmade Italian shoes.

Greyson was always amazed at how many bent cops made it so stupidly obvious by dressing so expensively. He didn't think he'd ever owned one suit that cost a quarter as much as any of those.

Had they been real, he would have run a hand down the front of one to confirm, but he knew they were silk or the finest wool. And impounded as evidence for now, if he really wanted to experience them first hand, back at the station.

Greyson shook his head and went back out into the main room, standing exactly in the center of the projected bed and facing the window he remembered somehow.

"There?" he asked, gesturing with his jaw.

"Yes," Rachel's mind had stopped her at the edge of the bed, like it was real. "Thought I hit him with a second shot as he went over the rail, but it didn't cause him to splatter on the pavement. Damn thing moved like a monkey."

Yes, her second shot had hit. A glancing kiss on his arm that required him to shift his feet to hands to make the climb down, else he would have splattered.

Greyson shook his head to clear it and turned back to the room.

Ethen knew exactly how to track down the other

Phrenic. Not the one that had killed Dominguez. He was already standing in the middle of the room looking at another cop with a big enough nerve scrambler to finish the job.

But he could give them Zaborra. The partner who had tossed Ethen into the role of a lifetime, sacrificing him unless he could survive the stubborn son of a bitch he was impersonating. Zaborra who had laughed when Ethen had suggested that the humans were more dangerous than just a shallow pool of guppies to feed on.

He had had his doubts before killing Leigh, but living inside the man had just convinced him how stupid he had been to ever come to this planet in the first place. How dumb a life of crime really was.

Ethen knew he could escape easily enough. Become someone else and walk aboard a transport. As long as he wasn't a Phrenic they might want to interrogate, he'd probably be fine. But where would he go?

Greyson Leigh was seductive. Powerful. Self-contained. Maybe what Ethen wanted to be when he grew up, if he could explain that to anyone who would listen longer than it took to shoot him.

Dare he just hide inside the man for the rest of their lives?

Hunter Bureau already knew there was a rogue Phrenic loose. Ethen had no reason to let them know that there were, in point of supreme order, two rather than one.

He'd lived Greyson Leigh for a week already, and it felt like years, struggling to keep the man from reaching up and somehow strangling his killer in ways that had only been stories mothers told rambunctious toddlers to keep them from misbehaving.

Be quiet and pay attention, or one of these days one of your victims will come back from the dead to get you.

He'd never believed it possible. Not then.

Greyson Leigh was curing him of that arrogance, one tiny drip of water at a time. Chinese torture, on the inside of his forehead. Athena, banging away with her brazen axe until she emerged fully grown and killed Zeus.

Greyson sucked in a hard breath and slowly turned in place, committing the room to memory. Over the memories he already had of the place when it was still furnished with more than projected magic.

Asher was playing it cool, standing silently off to one side, watching him like he was a great teacher she needed to emulate on her way to owning the boys and girls at Scotland Yard. There was something to it, over and above Greyson trying to keep his heart rate down and manageable.

Doing it this way imprinted the crime scene in your mind for later. Move through holograms to see things from strange angles. He could even smell the faint hints of ammonia in the air from where they had disinfected blood stains earlier.

Greyson reviewed the file in his head and turned to his new partner.

"So, Dominguez the Casanova of the Eastern Metroplex meets some girl at a bar?" he asked. "Sweet talks her back to his place. They had gone at it once on the bed, but he's got an appointment with you, so he checks his watch, realizes he's late, like usual, and tries to get rid of her before you get here?"

"That's the theory, boss," she said, looking around like he had done, slowly and deliberately. "Organic evidence of a sexual encounter, both on his body and on the bed. Two glasses of wine spilled in the struggle. One Phrenic running for his life when help accidentally shows up, or we might never have realized we had an infiltrator."

Greyson nodded. Ethen smiled inside.

It hadn't been that impressive. Man had a dick smaller than average for a human, but one of the advantages of being a shapeshifter was that you could resize things on the fly and rearrange bits to get the most pleasure for yourself, even out of a useless, self-absorbed shit like Carlos Dominguez, with his slicked back hair and gold jewelry.

Girl might as well enjoy herself before she eats your brains, right?

Dominguez would have never cured Ethen like Greyson did.

"There was nothing useful from the bar interviews in the files," Greyson said abruptly, stepping backwards in the crime. "Anything you remember that didn't seem important enough to list?"

He watched Rachel cast backwards in memory, eyes unfocused and shivering back and forth as she looked at things inside her head.

Cop eyes.

"No," she said after a few moments. "Dominguez was a regular in the place, one of about six meat markets where he usually found dates. Only two of them are gay bars, so the presumption was that the man was about a two on the Kinsey scale, rather than any higher number. Never really mattered, since he did his job and had no more than the usual civilian complaints."

"Tall blond with big tits walks in and she's fresh game?" Greyson nodded, walking her through the report she and Jansen had compiled, along with getting Zielinski himself into the field for a rare foray into copdom.

"You know Carlos," Rachel grimaced. "Anything that will slow down enough. Doesn't even have to actually stop running, just slow down. Bought her a couple of drinks. Whispered sweet nothings into her ear. A little dancing, a little grinding. Probably a blowjob in the taxi on the way here."

No, but a good presumption on Rachel's part. The man had been a little persistent, but Ethen had been more interested in getting him isolated. Too much risk he might blow his load in the car and then dump her with a pat on the ass before they got to his apartment.

Oh, yeah, Greyson knew Dominguez.

"But she's not human," Greyson completes the thought. "Phrenic has already killed the girl, absorbed her, and was setting a trap for Dominguez."

"Not that difficult a trap," Rachel sneered now, finally letting some personality show through the cop façade. "If you put a giant pencil sharpener in the wall behind a glory hole marked **Insert Penis Here** and told the man what it was, he'd probably still be convinced it would fail before his mighty dick did."

"You ever fuck him, Rachel?" Greyson asked.

Cop routine, but necessary here, and best that they covered it as part of the larger topic. It would change things if she had fucked the man, too. Not much, but some.

"Not for lack of offers," she growled in a terrible voice as she stared at him. "Probably catch things they don't even have names for yet in the worst South American barrios."

Greyson grinned. Ethen had absorbed enough memories off of Carlos before they fled to confirm the man's regular visits to the clinic and prophylactic treatments for every little thing that might come along. But yeah, Dominguez had probably tried everyone he could stick his dick in. Boring in bed, too, in spite of all the practice.

"So we'll skip the bar for now," Greyson said aloud. "She wasn't a regular, so nobody could mark her with anything worth following up on, and we've got a missing person's report two days later that matched up to security footage."

"Kelly Anne Nazarian," Rachel nodded. "Good time girl of no great note. Secretary at a law firm not that far from the bar downtown. Not much to go on."

"That's why she's the best target for something like this," Greyson and Ethen echoed in a strange, Greek chorus. "Right looks. Right attitude. If she somehow runs into someone she knows while she's letting Dominguez down her pants, nobody's going to really say anything, because she's already got a rep. Right or wrong, the interviews paint her as something of a slut, just like our boy Dominguez. Match made in hell, if you wanna look at it that way."

"You think she's that simple, Leigh?" Rachel's tone took on an edge that made him glance over sharply. "That any woman is?"

"Most of the time, no," he replied curtly. "But I've read the report you typed up. The interviews with her boss and a couple of her girlfriends. You honestly think that woman was deeper than a half-dry mud puddle, Rachel? Her whole life reads as one long party, interrupted by the need to go to work enough that she could afford prettier clothes to maybe attract a sugar daddy. Too bad she didn't meet Dominguez for real. She might have been shallow enough for him. He certainly was rich enough for her to want to latch onto."

"A cop?" Rachel laughed. "Rich? You gotta be kidding me."

"Follow. And learn," Greyson suddenly cracked the whip sharply on the young hunter, walking into that closet that was almost a quarter the size of Greyson's current studio apartment, all by itself.

"What do you see?" he asked from the deepest part, gesturing at the holographic rows of suits and shoes and life that were all in boxes downtown right now.

"Man liked to dress snazzy," Rachel replied carefully, aware that there was a trap lurking, but unable to see it yet.

Greyson nodded at his own realization. She'd grown up lower middle class, like him, so she had never really had a chance to appreciate money, always scrambling for it her whole life, and trying to live the kind of exemplary monastic existence that would get her a job in London in a few years. Never had so much spare that she could just blow it on anything, let alone clothes.

Greyson pointed to one of the suits, carefully not putting his hand through it.

"Handmade," he said. "Hong Kong or Rome. Don't know without actually looking at the tailor's label inside. Bespoke. Silk or wool, rather than polyester or something newer or cheaper. Stylish. Really nice suits that look good, even on a guy like Dominguez."

He waited for her to nod, acknowledging that much information, but still missing context. Obviously never bought a suit with or for a man. If they were going to be partners, he'd have to introduce her to a couple of tailors he knew.

Hadn't bought anything more than a shirt from either of them, but they made excellent contacts for understanding the finer details of clothing, which was something every cop needed in her repertoire.

Greyson went ahead and told Rachel how much just one of those suits would cost. Watched her eyes bug out for just the briefest moment. Observed as she silently counted the suits in the image and did the math in her head.

"Detective/Hunter makes about a third again more than you do, Patrolman," Greyson said darkly. "Throw in Universal Basic Income just because, and you go buy yourself this closet of fancy clothes. Yes?"

"Not without a sugar daddy who really loved me," she said in a tiny voice. "But Dominguez was always the sugar daddy to good time girls and rent boys."

Her voice kind of just trailed off, like it did when a cop suddenly had a flash of insight that leapt them over a logical chasm.

"So they weren't just rumors?" she asked after a moment. "He was that bent?"

Greyson shrugged most eloquently. The man was dead, and his cop sugar daddy had been sent to Florida to keep his mouth shut.

One of them, anyway. Greyson's old investigation had only just started getting to the interesting bits, back in the day. Lot of people had probably started getting twitchy when the Metropolitan brought him back.

"He might have had a fabulously wealthy aunt," Greyson said in a tone that mocked the very idea. "The kind that liked to make sure her favorite nephew always dressed well."

"Thirty was too old for Carlos," Rachel sneered. "Don't ever see him going after cougars."

"You didn't know the punk when he was barely older than you are now," Greyson said. "Let us just suggest that he grew more discerning and selective about age when he could afford to say no at a later date."

"When he was on the take."

Rachel had discovered anger.

Probably at herself for believing the stories Dominguez had told her privately, to deflect personal questions.

Cops recognize the need to keep a private life where police work doesn't intrude. Greyson had his synth whiskey and his classical music. Emelina when she had an itch nobody else could scratch.

He hadn't pried on Rachel, because she needed that same place, a white room in your mind where you could go strip naked and not be a cop for a while.

And she'd taken Dominguez's facile lies at face value.

Until she had to put her cop back on and peel the layers of that onion back, crying angry tears all the while.

"When he was on the take," Greyson agreed with her.

Before another cop started sniffing around from the far end of things and accidentally got close enough to make Zielinski—and Greyson's fellow officer—a little too nervous. Enough so that they'd framed him and gotten him fired to protect their house of lies.

Until Dominguez was dead, and couldn't be embarrassed anymore. And Zielinski was taking the fall but getting away clean. Commissioner Owens was currently walking a ledge on a very tall building.

"So how does all that impact our case?" Rachel asked after a moment to contain her rage.

Greyson grinned at her. Rachel had the makings of a fantastic cop. Just needed some seasoning and she'd be better than him in a couple of years.

"We're chasing a Phrenic killer," he said. "Simple thing. Straight-forward. If they stay put in somebody else's life, eventually they get tripped up by something. Usually they panic when we come sniffing around. Half the time, they run like hell and the lucky ones manage to get away, usually off-world where we don't have the authority to chase them."

"And the other half?" Rachel asked.

"Those are the ones Hunters like us kill," Greyson smiled.

"You think he's still around?" she asked.

"Let's go find out."

BECAUSE IT WAS STILL AN ACTIVE CASE BEING FOLLOWED at high enough political levels to make people involved nervous, the girl's apartment was closed off when Greyson got there to see it with his own eyes.

Kelly Anne Nazarian's roommate had been allowed to tell a female officer in uniform what clothing to stuff in a bag, given a stipend, and put up in a hotel until the Bureau allowed her back into her flat. Maybe another week, depending on Greyson's call.

Like with Dominguez, there was a uniform here at all times. Easy duty until Greyson decided that he didn't need the place locked down and isolated. The woman officer let them in and Greyson had another moment of déjà vu, but at least this wasn't as bad.

Ethen had stalked her, taken her, and used her to get to the cop, because those had been Zaborra's orders. When that failed, the freak had ordered him to go after Greyson. Take out the one cop that his memories from Dominguez said might be good enough to catch them. If the authorities didn't come, then he could at least hide out there for a while until Zaborra came up with a better plan.

Ethen growled inside when he realized that he had always been the follower, hanging on Zaborra's words and doing whatever the being ordered. And always taking the deadlier risks. Nothing he had ever done had ever been good enough for Zaborra.

Maybe it was Greyson talking, but he was suddenly sick of being the patsy all the time. In Greyson, he had maybe finally found a role model for how he could have lived.

Self-contained, rather than existing as a projection of someone else. Just being, instead of hurting people.

Phrenic weren't supposed to have mid-life crises, but Greyson suddenly looked back over a mental shoulder at him with those hard, gray-blue eyes, as if to say *Are you kidding me?* while shaking his head.

But Ethen was a cow in the abattoir chute now, being driven towards the big human with the bigger hammer. Taking all the serious risks while Zaborra was hiding as a food delivery driver, scoping out more interesting next targets he could go after while Ethen had to hold off the entire Hunter Bureau by himself.

About now, a man might get mad at that sort of treatment, Greyson seemed to say to him. Maybe it was Ethen's overactive imagination. And his fear.

He stepped into the apartment and looked around. Other than emptying out the almost vacant refrigerator unit, the officers hadn't done much to the place. Kelly Anne Nazarian wasn't important enough for Zielinski to take it all into evidence downtown so he could make things disappear before they came into the public record. Boxes that magically fell off trucks between here and there.

Shallow and flouncy. That had been the image of the woman that the interviews had painted. Tall and pretty and buxom, but didn't look all that much smarter than a houseplant.

Her and the roommate didn't have any pets. Greyson got the impression that Little Miss Kelly wasn't organized enough for someone else to rely on her. Harsh, he knew, but that was years of soldier and cop speaking. He had never had a dog because he had always kept such strange hours and didn't have someone else around that could give a mutt the love and attention they deserved.

Pinks. Yellows. Greens. Bright colors everywhere, like he had wandered into the room just after a cotton candy machine had exploded. Strips of gauze like wall hangings in strange locations. Generic art framed on the walls that looked vaguely surrealistic. Maybe by someone unwilling to actually commit to walking in Dali's footprints, but still trying to impress people.

Rachel followed him down the entryway, past several semi-stylish jackets or cloaks hanging on a coat tree with mostly complete pairs of shoes underneath, and into the living room.

The space was a close match, architecturally, to where Dominguez had lived. Bathroom close to the front door, like a hotel room. Kitchen. Dining space. Living room as you got deeper, with two bedrooms off the side. The roommate had the master bath.

She had been checked out and been cleared of being a suspect, once Zielinski's folks had subjected her to the sorts of examinations and psychological torture they did when they thought they might have a disguised Phrenic on their hands. DNA wouldn't show a deviation, but the Guild had given them other tools at the same time they allowed a few, trained humans to have nerve scramblers.

Those sorts of things weren't man-portable, or Greyson

would have had them with him and Rachel. Right now, he had his training, his instincts, and his new partner.

And a killer loose.

Rachel hadn't passed the Detective exam yet. Might never bother to take it. At the moment, she didn't have the prior experience to be allowed into the exam room, like he had, nor the degree she was pursuing.

Probably take London's exam instead and go over as soon as she blew it away and they offered her a job. And they would. Two more years and he'd have a peer, as well as a partner. At a minimum.

Greyson's ego wasn't so bad that he couldn't recognize Rachel's gifts, raw and unrefined as they were today. If he was still around in fifteen years, she might have ended up his Captain. Had she stayed. Or maybe come back, like he had.

"What are we looking for?" she asked now, following him into the living room.

This one still had furniture Greyson couldn't walk through, so he moved clear to the sliding glass door overlooking the tiny balcony and turned back to look around. Rachel was an arm away to his left, mirroring him.

"Playing a hunch," he said, reaching back deep into all those things the Army had taught him. How to get inside your enemy's head and predict his life and his escape routes, before you even tried to plan your assault.

Panicked men move like rabbits. Mindlessly. So the key is to know what path he'll aim for when he hears something, and plant your trap there.

"Carlos Dominguez is our target," he heard himself say aloud. "Detective/Hunter. One of the top cops in the Bureau, at least as far as hunters go. Kovalchuk was better, but he's dead. Jansen's a better killer, but he's not all that good a cop, a little too lazy to do all the legwork and building networks of informants. That's why he had you, to balance him out."

That last said as he turned his head over to watch the faintest hint of blush creep up her normally-dusky face. Rachel shrugged.

"So we somehow get inside information on the Bureau," Greyson continued slowly, almost absently. "Not sure who they talked to, or maybe Dominguez just has that big of a rep on the streets that they could get it from the corner green grocer. I'm sure there is another team looking for leaks back at headquarters, but that's probably being headed by Redhawk, so we don't need to worry about it."

"We don't?" she turned her head towards him now, rather than just absorbing the room.

"Edgar Redhawk is the dangerous one," Greyson nodded. "The rest of the folks on Six are politicians and flunkies. Edgar Redhawk is the only killer up there. He could come down to Four any time he wanted and fit right in with us."

"Got it," she said, turning back to the room.

"So we find out Dominguez's weakness," Greyson mused. "Like you said, probably about a two on the Kinsey scale, so we decide to use a girl as our Trojan Horse. Could have just as easily been a man, but we'll tentatively assume that our Phrenic has so-called feminine tendencies, at least as humans would classify it. That would make it easier to impersonate."

"So-called?" Rachel's voice had just a hint of razor-sharp sneer to it.

Greyson grinned.

"If we take the general position that feminine means softer, more pliant, more willing to go along with things, rather than aggressive and bossy," he said. "Present company excluded, of course, but more of a Twentieth Century model, or maybe Nineteenth."

Rachel Asher's grin was a thing of beauty as she caught the joke and nodded.

"Phrenic have genders, when they revert to mating form," Greyson continued. "We just so rarely see them that way that it's easy to forget. They look androgynous in the base form everybody knows, with those surface scutes protecting spots."

"Scutes?"

"Think sea turtles, Asher," Greyson said. "Those designs on their skin are actually a kind of a hardened cartilage as a layer of dermal armor. When they go for mating forms, they look like skinny, bald humans, but with human-like sexual organs, more or less."

"Right," she nodded. "So this one might be a girl freak instead of a boy, if you took her all the way back to the start?"

"Like I said, criminals make mistakes, but some of them aren't immediately obvious." Greyson turned to face closer to her now, a forty-five degree angle. She mirrored him. "But when they make choices, you can sometimes extrapolate outwards from there. So I'll start with that as a working theory."

"What does that give us?" she asked, head cocked a little in confusion, as if she couldn't quite see where the road was taking them.

Greyson stopped and considered the exact implications. Ethen reached a hand in and made sure that some words didn't get said, because that would give Rachel Asher too many clues. And she would ask the right questions.

Or the wrong ones.

Ethen suddenly realized that he didn't want to kill anyone else, ever again, just as much as he didn't want to die, so Ethen needed to dance this carefully. Greyson Leigh was dead and it was a great shame but nothing could bring the man back. Killing him had been something Zaborra ordered him to do, but Ethen was seriously considering hiding inside the man forever, if he could. It was a better life than he'd ever imagined he could live, as boring as the man was on the surface. But that was a cloak he wore around strangers.

No more Zaborra talking down to him.

Ethen just had to figure out how to betray Zaborra and get that bastard killed without blowing his own cover. And he realized now, looking back over the last several years, just how much he owed that son of a bitch.

"I'm not sure yet," Greyson finally said. "It was on the tip of my tongue, but it's gone now. I'm sure it will pop back out soon, once it has enough time to digest."

"So how'd they come to pick her?" Asher asked. "What brought this particular bimbo to the killer's attention? And why are they trying to replace Dominguez, anyway?"

"The second part's easier to guess," Greyson said. "Hunter Bureau gets called when a Phrenic or any other alien goes rogue and is too much for a simple beat cop to take down. Heavy Response Teams are great for hostage situations and kicking in doors, but you have to run your prey to ground and tree them first. For humans, that's easy enough for the regular divisions to handle. But he knows who's going to come after him, so he had to take one of us, one of you, out. Carlos was the one whose number came up."

"So somebody's watching Dominguez and figures his type," Rachel said. "Did they pick her up at some bar or party and bring her back here or take her to their place?"

"I'm guessing not here," Greyson said. "Home court advantage if you get the girl to come to your apartment, as long as she's not so crazy that knowing where you live is a liability. Kelly might have a roommate. She does. Might have a dog. She doesn't. Might have a stunner or a baseball bat hidden where she can fight back. Didn't look. Pretty sure we'll have to find our killer's lair, and we'll get DNA evidence she was there."

"So do you just hang out at one of those bars like Dominguez did?" Rachel asked. "Scouting the terrain once you figure out what makes Carlos go beep and then find her?"

"No," Greyson let his intuition speak now. "That takes too long and they've got to move fast to get to cover because the authorities have rumbled to them."

"They?" Rachel asked, glancing over.

"Him or her," Ethen said with Greyson's mouth quickly.

Any mistakes in front of good cops will get you killed, Ethen reminded himself.

Greyson stepped up now and shoved him politely to the side.

"What we are looking for is someone invisible enough to walk right up to her front door without setting off any alarms," he said. "A job that lets you move around, scouting people, without anyone actually noticing you're even there."

Ethen leaned back, aghast as Greyson started putting pieces together in front of him. Zaborra had always thought he was smarter than everybody else, Ethen included. Always going on about how his brains and the ability to disguise himself made him unstoppable.

It had been Zaborra's plan from the start. Ethen had argued half-heartedly, like he always did, but he always lost any argument with Zaborra.

It's called gas-lighting, pal, Greyson muttered at him. *Look it up*.

Ethen froze, a tiny deer in the middle of a dark road as headlights approached around a bend. He could feel Greyson Leigh slipping away from him and gripped the man as hard as he could.

Another fear gave him a sudden burst of strength.

Deathwalkers, the old legend called them. A victim that somehow broke loose of your control and evicted you from your own, Phrenic mind. Eventually, they lost control as well, but by then the host was uncontrollable and everything went zombie. Blood-thirsty, carnivorous monsters.

"So who can knock on the front door and nobody cares?" Rachel asked.

Ethen's panic doubled as he realized that he and Greyson had fallen silent with the internal struggle to suppress the cop, to keep him from looking over his shoulder to see what had become of him.

Hopefully, the silence could be played off as musing, and no parts of his body were accidentally changing shape, reverting to base form. Even looking right now would probably tell a killer like Rachel Asher everything she needed and he'd be dead in a second.

I don't want to die, he screamed internally.

We all will, Greyson's ghost snarled back at him.

That seemed to drop a blanket of calm over Ethen's entire being.

We will all die.

I could screw up right now and Rachel will kill me. That might even be for the best. No more killings on my part. No more victims. No more crime.

But that son of a bitch Zaborra will get away, just like Olek Zielinski's in the process of doing. If Rachel kills the freak, and everyone assumes there is only one, Zaborra's free to keep up his reign of terror.

Not on my watch, pal, both he and Greyson seemed to growl in unison.

A most bizarre Greek Chorus, standing in a hall of twisted mirrors.

Ethen re-energized his control of Greyson and distracted

the man with the need to stop Zaborra. That seemed to do the trick.

Greyson turned suddenly and marched into the kitchen, Rachel hot on his heels.

He stopped in front of the refrigerator and pulled it open. Completely empty when he looked, but he already knew that. Still, pieces came together like a jigsaw assembling itself.

"Tell me about the refrigerator," he ordered her, standing back upright but leaving the door open in his hand.

Rachel blinked for a few seconds, and then pulled out her handheld. Asher had a fantastic memory, to go with all the right instincts, but nobody held that level of detail in conscious thought.

Greyson was making her look it up rather than doing the work himself because that would stick with her on the next case, and the one after that. It would become part of those cop skills she taught to her young partners over in London, when she became him.

He watched Rachel spent several minutes reviewing logs and pictures before she spoke, but that was fine by Greyson. Preferable, even, because that meant she was assembling parts of the crime just as he had.

"Freezer contents heavy on ice cream, ice trays, and frozen meals you popped into the microwave," she said finally. "Fridge had to-go boxes from take out or delivery joints in the neighborhood. Spices and sauces in bottles. Chocolate bits and salsa in various containers. Several bottles of wine, mostly pinks."

"Nothing fresh," Greyson said. It wasn't a question. "No vegetables or fruit."

"Correct," Rachel agreed.

Just to be sure, Greyson moved to the stove unit. It was

an old-fashioned design dating back to his grandparent's era. Microwave over the stove top. Oven underneath.

One of these days, the Guild is going to sell us a microwave so advanced that nobody ever bothers to put a stove or oven into an apartment like this again, he mused.

Greyson pulled the oven door open and squatted down in front of it. Electric and thoroughly modern, unlike the ancient gas unit his grandparents had loved. Two racks, spotlessly clean. He ran a finger over them just to confirm, but he wasn't surprised.

Standing, he studied the stove top. Solid sheet of something that wasn't glass, but looked enough like it, with five circles on it indicating where burners lurked underneath like ancient submarines playing war games under the ice.

Again, the white glove inspection, although he wasn't wearing any. Clean. Not that hard to accomplish, since you could wipe it down easy enough, but there weren't any spots he could see where food had been permanently cooked into the surface.

"Never been used?" Rachel asked, following his logic.

"That's my guess," Greyson replied. "Maybe you spill something coming out of the microwave, but I'm pretty sure either you won't find any pots or pans in here, or if you do they're as pretty as the day they left the factory."

"Take out in the fridge," she repeated the detail.

"Tall, pretty, and dumb," Greyson replied. "Plus, she works at a law firm, so she had to dress nice and doesn't want anything to drip and risk ruining her clothes."

"Delivery driver," her eyes lit up huge.

"You asked who could just walk up to the front door and knock, and nobody would care," Greyson pointed out.

"Jesus," Rachel's voice got small. "Perfect cover, for someone who can become someone else."

"And it lets you hunt your next victim, scout the terrain, in almost perfect invisibility," Greyson said.

"Now what?" she asked.

"Now we go back to the station and ask the system to spit out another missing person's list, including occupation," Greyson sobered. "Let's go back two months, since we don't know when the Phrenic killer arrived."

"Can't we tighten it down some?" Rachel's face got scrunchy.

"I don't know if we have leaks at headquarters, Rachel," he grew grim. "A spy of some sort, feeding bits to outsiders. Especially if Zielinski's been tossed out on his ass. That man will still have friends that will want to protect him, even if just to cover their own asses when someone finally decides to go over the Captain's life with a microscope."

"And we filter the big list ourselves, not mentioning anything to anyone," she nodded, eyes suddenly bright with ideas. "Because we already know we're dealing with a freak, excuse me, a Phrenic infiltrator of some sort."

"And they can't shapechange themselves without a pattern," Greyson nodded. "They have to kill someone and take their form by absorbing their DNA, and they get their mind along the way."

"Where do the Phrenic come from, anyway?" she mused aloud.

"The Merchant's Guild has been remarkably evasive on that very topic," Greyson turned to face her fully. "I've never seen the evolutionary benefit of such a thing evolving naturally, but if you were doing some black magic genetic engineering, could you think of a better spy and assassin to make?"

"Vampires?" she asked.

"Something like that," he said. "You send them in and they kill a target, and then can impersonate them perfectly, at least for a while, if not forever. Mother Nature might not come up with that on her own, unless there were two intelligent species on one planet."

"If you look at a vampire as another species, those same sorts of thing work here," she said quietly. "We always thought that we were alone in the universe."

"Turned out we were just so far away from anybody else that it took a century for the signal to get there," Greyson completed the thought. "And then they came looking."

"But the Merchant Guild might not have been the first."

Rachel's awe was something to watch, because Greyson could see her attacking that question like a river deciding to go after a mountain. Drip by drip, peeling away a little at a time, until you had the inner truth revealed.

He didn't know any better than she did, but he also didn't care that much.

Greyson Leigh just needed to stop a killer.

"So we're going to the station and programming the search," he said simply. "Then you drop me at my place. Have the system print out the results on paper but don't grab them until the morning when you come get me tomorrow at seven. I know a great place for breakfast that I'm sure Jansen or Dominguez would never have taken you."

"The search will take all of about five minutes to run, Greyson," Rachel said with a mild exasperation. "Printing it another ten at the most."

"I want people looking over our shoulders, Rachel," he said, turning and walking out of the kitchen as she followed.

He took a long look around the rest of the space he could see from here and sighed a little. It would be so easy to tell the roommate that she could come back. There was nothing left here that he needed to know. It had just been another link in a chain that would lead him to the killer.

But that would give too much away to people that had a

vested interest in what one Detective/Hunter Greyson Leigh was up to. Things he didn't want revealed.

Not yet.

Rachel followed him to the front door in silence. Tense silence, but she had figured out that he was up to something and didn't want to tell her yet. A most bright woman.

Down they went to the car. As she pulled into the late night traffic, Greyson studied her profile. Young, but dangerously smart. Raw, but she'd be a better cop than him in another decade.

"Here's the other piece, Rachel," he said in a low voice, once they were alone.

She didn't look, but her ears would have rotated at him like radar antenna, were she a cat.

"If they could get to Dominguez so easily, the killer had to have had help somewhere," Greyson said. "Leak, spy, something. Maybe one of the people Dominguez was leaning on for protection money decided they wanted the man dead. Nobody was going to bring me back, at least until Metropolitan Upkins got involved and stepped on a lot of toes to do it."

Rachel glanced over under hooded brows, but kept silent. Absorbing his copness, probably, which would just make her better.

"So I got enemies at the station," he continued. "We all do, but I don't know who all of mine are just yet. Hopefully, you aren't on that list, because I'd like to see you teach those limeys how to be better cops, and I'm pretty sure Upkins is expecting some of the people out there to be too dumb to pass up the chance to take a shot at me. She's the one that will be shooting back, not me."

Again the pause, watching her process it all. It was a gamble, but she had hopefully only been learning from Dominguez how to be a cop, and not a corrupt one.

"Stalking horse," she more or less whispered.

Greyson nodded.

"I think we've made a big jump in maybe solving this case," he said.

"But if we only ask the system for missing persons who worked as delivery drivers and such, then somebody might tell somebody, and then maybe our Phrenic catches word," she said with a nod he could only classify as methodical.

Working out the pieces to the jigsaw.

"And then he vanishes on us," Greyson said.

He turned back to watch the traffic out the windshield for a bit.

"I'd really like this to be a surprise," he whispered.

[9]

NIGHT

Greyson hadn't even bothered to get ready for sleep. He was Hunting now, and knew that his body had already shifted to another mode, where he only needed about three or four hours of sleep to get by. At least for several weeks.

The Army had pounded that into him. Or maybe he'd always had it and they were just the ones that found it. Polished it. Honed it to a fine, killing edge.

His clock read a little after one. The city was quiet, but not silent. Greyson was at his table, folded down from the Murphy bed, thinking about tomorrow.

There was already a stack of papers most likely waiting patiently in the middle of Rachel's desk for her to come retrieve them in the morning. It would have been nice to review the interior security tapes from tonight, just to see who happened along and took a look at the query across the top.

Idle curiosity, you know. Rachel's partnered with the great Greyson Leigh. I thought that maybe I could learn something about how to be a better cop.

It would even sound plausible, however full of shit the person talking would be.

Didn't matter at this point. Greyson knew there would be enemies, on Four as well as on Six. Or maybe the folks on Four taking quiet orders from the ones upstairs, orders that never seemed to make it into a log or database. Honest mistakes.

He grinned and watched the night drift by out the window. Boston never slept, since it was part of the Eastern Metroplex these days. Forty-odd million people crammed together in towers and transit tunnels. You could get all the way to DC itself, down at the south end and even into the place that had once been called Virginia, without ever emerging into sunlight.

Or night.

As he had told Rachel just before she dropped him off, most criminals are lazy. They'd rather cut corners than follow the rules, or they wouldn't be criminals in the first place. You just had to look for those spots and trace them forward and backward until you had all the pieces and could predict where to set your trap.

Greyson knew he was playing a hunch, but it felt right, going back over all the years he had hunted other people to death, with or without a badge to hide behind. His gut told him that there would be a nobody who worked part time as a delivery driver for one of the local restaurants or networks. Man had just disappeared about ten days or so ago and a girlfriend or a parent or maybe wife would file a report, but wasn't important enough that anyone had done anything beyond making next of kin file a report into the system, along with relevant personal information. Maybe he had just walked. Maybe he had even come back. That was what the paper was to check.

Greyson knew, if he wanted to check that there would be

another body before that, or perhaps not. Maybe the killer had come to Earth in a good enough disguise, and the driver was his first kill in Boston. Maybe not.

Again, didn't really matter. When dealing with a Phrenic, you had a chain of bodies and missing persons that you tracked, until either you cornered the bastard, or he caught a whiff of cop and ran like hell for the off-world.

Right now, Greyson was holding the last glass of synth whiskey before he took the bottle in, and working a case where a *skinwalker*, to use Zielinski's slur, had killed Carlos Dominguez, but been interrupted trying to absorb him.

Rachel had believed she had chased the monster off, at least until Greyson had explained to her just how lucky she had gotten.

"But I shot him, Leigh," she had insisted.

"With a palmstunner, Asher," he had countered. "You're lucky the damned thing panicked and ran."

"Why?"

The compact anger that fueled the woman had been visible underneath at that point.

"A Phrenic is strong enough that it had already killed Dominguez," Greyson had noted. "Broke his neck with its bare hands, Rachel. Palmstunner just gave him a jolt, but he could have just as easily come off the ceiling at you as gone the other way trying to escape."

"Oh."

Maybe she had finally discovered her own mortality at that moment. If so, it would just make her a better cop long term, because good Hunters needed to sneak up on their prey, rather than being able to rely on kicking in a door and arresting everyone in the room.

That's what separated them from the other cops. What made them hunters.

And why he had a nerve scrambler in his holster, resting

next to the empty bottle of whiskey on the table. Had he not been so surprised when Zielinski showed up, he might have been more careful a few hours later, when Emmy knocked. But he hadn't started assembling the case at that point.

She could have been the rogue Phrenic, walking right up to his door and knocking, but someone would have had to read a most complete file on the life of Greyson Leigh to put all those pieces together and know how to get him like that.

So why had the Phrenic not killed Rachel? As he had said, turning right instead of left and it could have landed atop her like a pouncing mountain lion so fast she never got a second shot off.

Posit: Not a hardened psychopathic killer, like so many of the worst of their kind turned into. This felt more like an amateur play, thinking they could outsmart the cops and infiltrate the Bureau.

That was exactly the sort of thing someone had designed the species for. The US Army had once done the same to a punk kid named Greyson Leigh. Become your enemy in thought. Outthink him and get inside his decision curves so you can predict his reaction to your attack and drive him where you needed him to be.

No, they weren't all that different, once you got deep enough.

So the guy panics. Goes out the window and down the fire escape.

Then what?

He's been blown. People have seen Kelly with Carlos, and the news will broadcast her image everywhere within a few hours with *Warning: Armed and Lethal* across the bottom.

Where does he go?

Option One: he grabs someone at random, just to kill them for a face to hide behind.

Greyson hadn't mentioned that piece to Rachel yet, but

that was why they had the whole printout, without any filters. For a town like this, it was probably nearly one hundred pages long, covering two months to the present. While she was looking for drivers, he'd be looking for random murders that looked like muggings gone wrong in the vicinity of Dominguez's death. The body would still be there afterwards, but now maybe you had mirror images, one walking around and one dead.

Not finding something close and sticking out like a sore thumb would lead him and Rachel to Option Two, which felt more likely right now. He reverts to his delivery driver and continues to look for more prey.

No body has been found, because that blows your cover, just like Kelly Anne is still officially missing, presumed dead, body *To Be Recovered*, maybe. So maybe the Missing Persons has been canceled when the guy walks back into his life and claims it was a bender, or a surprise trip to London Metroplex or maybe Florida Metroplex.

They aren't vampires, Rachel. They're spiders. Haul the corpses to their lair and keep them handy so they can swap shapes back and forth if they need to. Maybe another bimbo with big tits, if that's what it takes to seduce someone like Greyson Leigh, now that he's on the case and doesn't know about Kelly. Except he would, so they'd have to find someone else and replace her.

But that delivery driver is probably the next corpse over, drained dry like a desert mummy and sitting on a rack as insurance.

Greyson took a sip and contemplated what kind of a lair a Phrenic spider might need.

NIGHTMARES

Ethen dreamed, but now he was trapped inside the body of Greyson, and the man had broken free of his control.

It wasn't supposed to happen like that. You absorbed them, DNA and memories, when you sucked out all that fluid. A Phrenic could reshape itself then, imprinting a new life over the old one, like putting on a cloak.

But Greyson Leigh had been too much to control. Still waters running so deep that Ethen had accidentally drowned in them, unable to make it back to shore.

Now he was in dark, cold water, splashing about and feeling wet fingers claw at his legs.

Zaborra was there, standing on a nearby cliff just a little out of reach, up at the side of the pool where Ethen couldn't climb out. Looking down from safe ground. The son of a bitch was standing there laughing. Looked like a young Russian guy, but Ethen wasn't fooled.

Around him, something else was swimming with deliberate strokes. Circling at a distance. Playing with him by just making these wide, lazy loops, scrolling slowly inward like an ancient vinyl LP album record playing the first notes of something that would end up with Ethen being chomped at the end.

Music started. Greyson Leigh hummed the ominous theme to a shark movie, like a brass heartbeat, coming ever closer. Ethen tried to swim away, but every direction he turned he saw that triangular fin cutting the water, cutting off his escape.

Zaborra laughed.

The fin vanished into the water.

Ethen turned right and left trying to find it. Rachel was standing up there next to Zaborra, holding a nerve scrambler, but she wasn't going to shoot either of them. Just watch. She put on a bobby hat and smiled wickedly down at him.

"Cheerio, Governor," she called with a merry laugh.

Zielinski was on Zaborra's other side, holding a brass ashtray in one hand and a mighty Cuban cigar in the other. He puffed the coal of the cigar red hot and blew out a long stream of smoke that filled Ethen's face and lungs.

Dominguez was there. Naked with that small dick sticking out like a thumb and a beaver pelt of fur on his chest, like some tall, skinny Homo Australopithecus with a set of gold chains rattling around his neck as the man capered.

The music got louder, but the fin was gone.

Ethen looked down and saw the monster emerging from the darkest of those still waters, a Megalodon shark so big that it could eat a bus. The mouth opened with a chilling smile as it came up into bright moonlight, and then the beast bit him in half, shaking the pieces from side to side like a terrier with a rat.

Greyson woke from a terrible nightmare and nearly leapt out of bed for his gun before he finally realized he was back in his studio. The clock read four thirty, and that was good enough. He'd be an hour just burning off enough energy to sleep, and it wasn't worth trying.

Instead, he wiped his face and sat up, throwing the thin blanket to the bottom of the bed. Sweat drenched him and the bedding, so he stripped it as he stood up and left it in a pile on the floor.

The Murphy bed got folded up for now. He'd worry about putting new sheets on it tonight. Right now, he needed some coffee and some air, so he pulled the table down and slid the chair out from the corner where he stored it.

If Rachel wasn't going to be here in a few hours, Greyson might have gone ahead and just started his day. Gotten dressed and walked to one of the local joints for the kind of hearty breakfast that would fuel him for the day.

He started to pull down his coffee altar, but realized his hands were still shaking too hard to make things work, so he put it right back up in the cupboard and went looking for his pants. The gun had been in his off hand almost since before he was awake, and it stayed there for reasons he couldn't explain.

Just got dressed one-handed while keeping his eyes on the fire escape, as if there was a Phrenic killer out there, watching for his chance to slip into Greyson's apartment and try to kill him in his sleep. From the nightmare, it might have succeeded.

Or something.

Shirt next, Greyson had to rest the nerve scrambler on the table long enough to button things, and then he picked it up again.

What the hell is wrong with you?

He couldn't remember nightmares so vivid since he had left the army. Those were a good part of the reason he had gotten out, rather than staying on to make a thirty year pension.

A killer who can't sleep through the night eventually cracks. Better to be a cop and let things settle down. You aren't twenty-three any more, bulletproof and lethal. Let the kids do the stupid shit for a while.

About the time his hands wanted to tie a tie, Greyson found his center. He laughed as his mind and body automatically went to the rack in the closet that didn't have any ties on it anymore.

All burned, just like yesterdays should be.

Shoes laced and ready for combat, he grabbed his longcoat and went out the front door of his studio and down the stairs. Five AM. Boston just waking up and maybe thinking about putting coffee on. Or maybe going to bed for a few hours so you could stagger to your desk only a little late and hope nobody called a surprise meeting at nine to share some great news.

Hunters didn't punch clocks, but Rachel would be here in two hours for a master class in how to seduce a Phrenic murderer into dying at the hands of the police, instead of escaping to kill again.

He could get some coffee in him, and use that to calm himself to the point that he would look normal when she arrived. Nothing about the case should be making him this jumpy, but Greyson figured it was just the shock of returning to the old job.

All the old stuff being churned up from the dark depths where it has settled over the years. Being a cop again was like sticking a rake down there and mucking.

Bad stuff to plague his dreams, at least for a while.

Once that Phrenic was done, hopefully it would all go back to normal.

If there was such a thing.

$$[\ 11\ ]$$

RACHEL

Greyson had spotted the car when he was walking back to his apartment. Late model Chandler Jouster, parked half a block past the doorway to his part of the tower. Rachel Asher would be behind the wheel with the doors locked, reading her homework or something.

HE looked around to see if there were any other suspicious-looking vehicles on the curb somewhere. Sun was far enough up that joggers had been a nuisance on the sidewalks coming back and people were starting to go to work.

Still, a Jouster stood out, mostly because most cars these days were smaller, built for two. Moms and Dads still drove big boxes that could haul kids around if they had that many, or small four-doors if they didn't. Jousters were meant for four adults, and could haul six in a pinch. Usually, it was only three, with two cops up front and a handcuffed perp in back, silently glowering in a way that wouldn't compromise the rights Greyson had previously explained to them if they had the sense God gave a goose.

There. Almost as good as clockwork. Smaller Chandler,

maybe a Scout, but it was hard to tell them apart from this distance. Greyson had never been that much of a gearhead. It stuck out for being too clean in this neighborhood.

Greyson had occasionally checked a sneaker car out of the motor pool when he needed it for surveillance, but the first thing he always did with them was find an empty gravel lot somewhere and do donuts to kick up dust and throw muck and crap on the sides. Mechanics back at the office always bitched, but nobody ever looked twice at him on stakeout.

Greyson wondered who had followed Rachel this morning, and if she even knew they were there. Cop 101, but those folks had learned it as well as she had. Still, he checked his watch. Old-fashioned beast with gears driving each other from a battery that would probably outlive him, rather than the solid-state electronics most people preferred, if they even bothered.

Handheld told time just as accurately.

Ten minutes to seven. He could chirp her, or just start walking that way now and see how good her personal sensors were. Window rolled down as he took his first step and she waved once, closing up immediately.

Greyson nodded and trooped over. The passenger door unlocked as he got close, so he climbed in and slammed it shut. She was dressed almost identical to how he was, except she had a sedate gray tie on over her blue shirt and under her collar. Like him, longcoat in brown rather than a blazer, but hers looked nicer. Less miles and firefights on it, one presumed.

"Watchers behind us," Rachel said before he even started fastening the seat belts into place. "Picked them up not far from the station. Figured they were why you had me walk this particular path this morning, so I didn't bother losing them on the way over."

She looked over expectantly, with a matronly smile that was just a little frosty. The smart kid in the front row answering questions for the rest of the class that had been too lazy to read the homework.

Greyson nodded and finished his contraption.

"Turn left at the light and go down six blocks," he said simply. "We'll take a right then and hop up on the highway for a bit. Nice and casual."

"Still not trying to lose them?" she asked as the car eased into traffic.

"Want to know who cares that much," he replied, giving her the address and the freeway exit she needed to take. "Might be anybody, but without Zielinski, they're probably reporting to Owens at this point, at least indirectly."

"And we still don't know nothing, so we have this huge stack of dead trees to go through to try and find our first clue?" Rachel grinned.

"Fun part comes if I suddenly decide to have a loud Eureka moment in the restaurant, wave a piece of paper in the air too fast for optics to zero in on it, and then we high tail it out of there like the world was ending," Greyson grinned back. "Imagine the panic when they think we've gone from nothing to a major breakthrough they missed, and now have to somehow bump into us to catch up."

He picked up the stack of papers in the envelope between them, pulled them out, and inspected the top page.

"You didn't cut the deck yet, did you?" he asked.

"The what?" she glanced over.

The report was by date of disappearance, and then alphabetized within each day. Someone running the same report, or making a copy of it last night, would have the exact same stack with him, probably in the lap of whoever was sitting in the passenger seat of that Scout back there. The one that had lit out after them and was maintaining a polite distance.

Greyson didn't figure they could actually lose another cop. Most likely, someone wanting to follow Rachel would go ahead and drop a tracker on this car when she left it in the underground garage, and could then watch her drive around on their little navigation console.

But they wouldn't be able to listen in to a conversation in a random restaurant from outside. They'd have to come in and get within his line of sight to be any sort of social threat.

Assuming Rachel was clean and not just writing up reports for Zielinski and Owens in her spare time. She'd been a straight-arrow cop a year ago. And Greyson didn't think she was willing to bend too much if she really wanted London.

Once there she might bend, but that wouldn't be his problem at all.

All that flashed through his mind as he pulled the stack out, randomly pulled the top third off and put it on the back before sliding it right back into the envelope and putting it back.

"More mind games," he said happily. "If they have the same stack, and see me flip to a certain page, they can guess close."

"But you won't be starting on day one," she said. "So they'll be someplace completely messed up. Why are we working so hard to screw with other cops, Leigh?"

"It's my case, Rachel," Greyson let some of his anger show. "I had a nice retirement going, and those bastards decided to come mess it up. Zielinski had to walk out of the mist and sit down at my table. Threaten me. Cajole me. Finally make a deal with me. Cost him everything, because Upkins called my bluff and retired the son of a bitch. But she hasn't cleared the rest of the riff raff out of the building, so now, on top of everything else, I got angry cops afraid that

I'm going to start up the old investigations that nearly got them in trouble a year ago. Maybe jail time. So yeah, I'm gonna screw with them until I suss out which ones are trouble."

"And me?" she asked, glancing over as they accelerated up the ramp.

"If you're one of them, then nothing I do here is going to matter," Greyson stared hard at her, waiting for some flinch, some tell that would give her away. "Most likely, they'll fuck up the case and flush the Phrenic before I'm ready to take him down. So he runs. Probably gets away. I work for a while until it becomes clear that I can't solve the case, and then probably somebody big makes me a deal to retire again. This time for good."

"And if I'm clean?" she asked, angrily grinding the words out of a tense jaw like a Russian speaker. Like maybe she was a touch insulted at his presumption. As she should be.

"Then we have a chance to be heroes, kid," he said. "Simple as that. I come back as a favored son. You get dipped in honey and glory so deep your hair turns strawberry blond and the folks in London start stalking you about maybe coming over a bit early. So I don't care if you were a little bent. Or were even two days ago. You can go straight right now and help me solve the case, as long as you haven't spilled my lead to those two bozos back there. If you have, then you might as well just hit the next off-ramp and drop me at a bus station, because the case will be blown, regardless of what promises they made you."

She flinched.

Barely a twitch, but she might as well have screamed in the close confines of the car. And they both knew it.

Greyson watched her turn crimson all the way to the pointy tips of those cute ears. Noted the death grip on the steering wheel turning her knuckles white. Listened as she didn't breathe.

"Who?" he asked, skipping over all the other questions someone else might have asked. All the denials, evasions, and acceptance necessary to get to the critical point.

Jesus, was he going to have to walk every cop he knew through the stages of death on this case? Kubler and Ross probably owed him royalties at this point.

Still, she remained tightly focused. Silent. Angry now, if he was reading her eyes right. Wasn't sure if it was at him or someone else.

"Rachel?" Greyson pressed one last time.

If she didn't answer, he would just open his door at the next red light and walk into the crowd on the sidewalk. Maybe mail his badge and gun back in, just to be a shit. Because if Owens was in on this, he was so screwed he'd be wasting everyone's time even trying at this point.

Those morons would be tracking down every delivery driver and cross-referencing God knows what. Some fool of a detective, not even a hunter, would start interviewing them about Kelly Anne Nazarian and the target would vanish into the mists, like Greyson had done to Olek, back at the noodle bar.

"Redhawk," she finally admitted in a tiny voice.

Greyson sighed. That was that. Owens's right hand. Case closed, they just haven't told everybody yet.

"And Upkins," Rachel added just as she started down the off-ramp that would dump him onto the streets and back into civilian life.

Greyson stopped his motion to undo his seat belt and turned back to her.

"What?" he asked in a dead voice, just a hint above a whisper.

"Someone was watching us at the station house," Rachel

said, her own voice joining his in the graveyard. "Watched us leave. Counted the clock. Those two were standing there in my parking garage when I got home. Said they didn't think I would react well if they were in my living room when I walked in."

"Good way to get yourself killed," Greyson breathed.

"You have no idea," she rasped back. "I have to look in every closet and cupboard when I get home, gun in hand, just in cast somebody's already there."

"Oh, I know exactly what you mean," Greyson countered. "Nightmares this morning got me up at four-thirty. Went and got some coffee and came back to wait for you. Tell me about your visitors."

Stalking horse. But whose? Upkins changed the equation in his head. Had Redhawk seen that Owens was going down, and maybe move up and join the Metropolitan's staff instead of a lowly Police Commissioner? Or was he maybe maneuvering himself to replace the man completely?

Greyson felt the tides suddenly turn and start to run a different direction from what they had been just yesterday.

"Edgar Redhawk can be quite charming, even when he looks like he's sizing you up for a coffin," Rachel replied hollowly, as if she was standing a million miles away. "He did most of the talking. Interrogating."

Greyson grunted. That man would. Needing to impress the new boss that he could be salvaged when Owens had to take a fall, early retirement just like Zielinski had been offered. Assuming nobody had enough axe to grind to put the man in a cell for a while. Or another coffin.

"But he was there with Upkins?" Greyson confirmed.

"Yeah," Rachel's voice shook a little now, like maybe she'd had all that ugliness at the start of the night and it had only made its way over to his place later. "Wanted to know what you knew, with just two days on the case. I got the impression that she was expecting you to have already solved it by tomorrow."

"What did you tell her?" Greyson asked pointedly as the light turned green and she drove across the intersection and down into the city streets of the old west side. "Exactly."

"That you had a pretty good lead, but needed to sleep on it," Rachel said.

He watched her for another flinch and didn't see one. Didn't mean she wasn't lying. Maybe she was getting better at it.

Or Metropolitan Denise Upkins and her new assassin had maybe scared the young woman more than Greyson Leigh's reputation might.

"And?" he pressed.

"And that we were running a background query that you thought would narrow down your suspects pretty quickly today, after you had a chance to look at the missing persons for the last two months. Nothing else. I was too frightened by the power play I was seeing in front of me to try to come up with anything interesting on the fly."

"Good," Greyson nodded. "They'd have nailed your hide to the wall eventually for any lies. Let them come after me later. I'm a big boy. I can take it."

"Redhawk's turning?" Rachel asked/guessed.

"He's going to burn Owens," Greyson guessed aloud. "Maybe already has, and they just haven't pushed the man off the ledge yet. I'm guessing they told you to keep everything quiet."

"Redhawk did," Rachel's voice had a different edge now. Fear. "Upkins just smiled and said it wouldn't matter who knew. She knew you'd figure this out?"

"Something like that," Greyson said. "We have a history, she and I, going back many years."

"Anything you're going to tell your new partner?" Rachel glanced over.

"Nothing I'd tell even my shrink or my rabbi," Greyson shot back.

"You aren't Jewish," Rachel said.

"Exactly my point, youngster," he said. "Park here and take several deep breaths before you get out of the car. I need you looking natural and feisty today when we eat breakfast, since we'll have an audience watching."

"Redhawk's people?" Rachel asked.

"No," Greyson mused. "If they approached you last night, they'll expect you to keep them at least sort of up to date, but clear things with me before you leak it to them, so I can predict the incoming fire. That Scout back there is a couple of Vice Detectives or something. Somebody we won't know on sight, that owe favors to our boys. Any cop that walks in will be telling Zielinski and Owens everything they see. Keep that in mind."

"Got it," she said. "Incoming fire?"

"This case is just a wedge, Rachel," Greyson replied. "Upkins is likely to have other heads on stakes outside her office by the time you and I deliver her a Phrenic serial killer."

She nodded at him and took a deep breath.

Greyson watched Rachel move towards calm and wondered just how much house-cleaning Denise Upkins had decided to do under the guise of bringing him back onto the force.

It wasn't going to be pretty.

[12]

MISSING

GREYSON HAD ASKED FOR A TABLE INSTEAD OF A BOOTH, then taken a seat that let him see both the kitchen area and the front door. Rather than be across from him, he had Rachel on his left, watching the parking lot out the front.

The place was ancient. It had been a restaurant for more than a century for a while one of those big, national chains that never closed, with bright, airy interiors and a long counter where a single like Greyson Leigh frequently sat, reading the news on his handheld and sipping the coffee dark and heavy enough to stand a knife up in it some mornings. These days, it was a local joint, serving a better quality of slop than the chain had done because they didn't need to serve the exact same meals elsewhere. Texans had weird ideas about breakfast.

Waitress approaching knew Greyson's face but not his crimes. Taller woman, heavy-set with middle age and dyed hair needing work on the roots coming in. Dressed in the standard uniform of a skirt and apron, with a hat in her hair that always reminded him of a cloth tiara.

Greyson got the impression that she thought this might

be some sort of a date, rather than business, but he chalked that up to the woman not being able to smell cop coming off him this morning. Rachel didn't look like a cop or a prostitute. Wasn't dressed well enough to be an office drone, but too nice to be a machinist. Too sour and focused to be a girlfriend out for breakfast, and not rigid enough to be a tumble-and-food-before-parting sort of thing.

So the waitress decided to play it safe, from the smile she gave him.

"Coffee?" the woman asked, big glass carafe in one hand held up expectantly.

Greyson already had his mug flipped. Rachel was there a beat slow, but he put that down to her still recovering from expecting him to walk at that red light back there.

Which just might have taken her career down when he did.

Fuel got poured. Menus were left. They were alone.

"So I still can't tell," Rachel murmured finally when she realized he wasn't going to speak first. "Did I fuck up or not? With Redhawk and Upkins."

"We'll see," Greyson replied, about as honest as he could right now. "Pretty sure those two had you in an impossible situation last night. She's good about picking the death ground she wants to fight on, and very few people ever win when she decides to go all in."

"But?"

"If you told them I had a lead and needed to look at faces on that print out, and nothing else, then we might still solve the case," he looked over at her and felt the muscles in his face turn sour and brooding. Couldn't be helped.

Ethen nodded to himself, aware that even Zaborra wasn't so stupid as to stay with that cover if a Homicide Detective showed up out of the blue. He'd flee, probably just abandoning Ethen on this damned planet so that Zaborra could get home, thoroughly chastened.

Or not, the being didn't do introspection worth a damn. Would have made a lousy cop.

Ethen would have no chance to escape if that happened, at least until he found a way to slip the bonds of Greyson Leigh and vanish as well. Or he could stay.

Living with the man had opened his eyes to all the stupid shit that Ethen had ever done, and the raw luck that had kept him alive this long. And he had looked up gas-lighting as a verb on Greyson's handheld. Read the definition with their eyes.

He'd been a schmuck. A loser. A dupe that Zaborra had manipulated. But Ethen Boli had always been a victim. A sucker that a stronger personality could bully into taking risks for him.

Ethen Boli could never undo the crimes he had done. The murders that ruined so many other lives. Even putting the nerve scrambler in his mouth and pulling the trigger right now wouldn't fix that.

Plus, he needed to stop Zaborra first. End that creature's reign of terror in the shadows.

Then maybe he'd kill himself. End both his and Greyson's lives in one blast of retribution.

If he could.

Ethen knew he was a coward under it all. Looking at Greyson Leigh in the mirror had stripped away any lies or deflections he might have told himself otherwise. Listening to the man's internal monologue about how to be a good cop and a good person just laid it all bare, with no place left for an alien intruder to hide.

Hell, there were times the thought of letting Greyson just take over sounded better, but that was all the gas-lighting talking. The thought that Ethen Boli wasn't good enough, wasn't smart enough to ever be an upright citizen.

That way lay Deathwalkers.

"I'm clean, Greyson," Rachel said in a quiet, earnest voice.

It took both of them a moment to find context. She was referring to Upkins.

Greyson flashed back nearly a decade to a younger cop and a younger pol. The quiet things that had never quite erupted into a proper affair, but always danced right along those edges, even less frequent physical moments than he and Emmy had but just as intense.

For Denise, too much risk in opening herself up emotionally after her husband had died suddenly, balanced against certain needs, in a situation where a quiet cop who could keep his mouth shut might be enough.

Hadn't been that many occasions. And they had ended sharply when it became clear that she was poised to run for Metropolitan. And would likely win.

Even then Greyson had to remain in the shadows, or folks might have started to ask what he used to do for the Army. Answers he could not give without doing time in a military prison. Any scandal that was his would have stained her as well.

So they had parted.

Denise hadn't remarried, but maintained a different life now, dating famous people at a light-enough, arms-length kind of level, at least until she retired and could look out for herself and not just her career. Greyson had interviewed Emelina as part of a hunt that never got that close to the woman, but she had sought him out later. Just like Denise had.

Hunting the hunter.

Greyson nodded and looked at Rachel with searching

eyes. Finding the truth at the core of her soul, which was one of the things that made hunters able to see a Phrenic in human guise.

"The entire case hinges on that, Rachel," he said simply, in that quiet, methodical voice that penetrated stone like water finding any gap. "There isn't anybody else in the Bureau I trust not to fuck it all up, so stay clean."

The waitress returned before Rachel could reply. He might have timed it that way, though he would never admit it to anyone. Just smiled at her as realization dawned.

Greyson ordered heavy. Enough calories that he might have needed a nap later, but he didn't think they would get a chance at lunch or dinner unless the case was already screwed. Rachel listened and did the same.

He had an image in his mind's eye. The scent of heavy, greasy breakfast and morning bodies in the restaurant around them just reinforced that expectation of a delivery driver knocking on the woman's door with bags of food and smiling at her as she opened it.

She really had been a gorgeous woman from the pictures he'd seen, just as shallow as a pane of glass and about as transparent. Skinny like a volleyball player, but without any of the muscles or hunger that burned in those women. Chirpy laugh, big tits bolted on later, and a barely-leashed libido.

Yeah, she might have been perfect for a guy like Dominguez to keep on the payroll, along with the other mistresses Greyson presumed. Zielinski had certainly had one for every day of the week, back in the day.

But she was dead now. Gone. An empty husk kept in an underground lair by a trapdoor spider that emerged into the fading afternoon to hunt.

Except Greyson had no idea how he knew that. It was almost like he could see that place in the sewers, an old blocked off set of steam tunnels that had once connected buildings around a business campus.

The place the hunter went when he needed to sleep. Where he kept his bodies.

Greyson shook his head to clear it, but the image wouldn't go away. He almost felt like he had been in those tunnels at some point, perhaps even recently, a walking nightmare comparable to the one that have driven him from his apartment earlier.

Rachel had lapsed into silence, sipping her coffee and eyeing that manila folder on the table between them like it contained a bomb, or a poisonous spider. Greyson reached out and pulled it closer, flipping it open and pulling out the stack.

"Cop just walked in," Rachel said clearly without moving her jaw.

Greyson didn't flinch. Didn't look up. Just kept his face bent over and let his peripheral vision find the shadow by the front door.

"One?" he asked quietly.

"So far, yes," she said. "Don't recognize him."

"Don't stare," Greyson ordered her. "Let go of the man and just mark where she seats him."

She turned towards him now and sipped her coffee.

"Do we all look so obvious?" she asked after a second.

He looked up and grinned at her.

"Cop has a walk, Rachel," he said. "That's why so few can make it undercover for long. Or be hunters. You have to blend in and all those years of hiding behind that badge make you stand out."

"Invulnerability," she noted. "That's what it is. Nothing can touch me, because I have a gun and a badge."

"Yup," Greyson grinned. "Problem is, some of them begin to believe that, and so they start to bend. Little decisions to cut a few corners. They add up. Bad ones decide after a while that the world owes them something extra for putting up with all the shit the job brings. For the bodies that have to be mopped up after taking a concrete dive, or when someone pulls a weapon and makes you kill them. After a while, all those little things start to turn into big things."

"Closets full of silk suits," she grimaced.

"Exactly," he agreed. "Dominguez was an end-case example of why you need Internal Affairs watching everyone and hating all cops, or they'll get bent too and then everything goes to hell because the police stop doing that protect and serve bit, and start protecting their own from the laws. People on the streets can smell that, so they start hating cops and it becomes a vicious cycle."

"How do we break it, Greyson?" she got thoughtful now.

"If it was up to me, I'd make everyone be a cop for about five years, and then make them move on," he said. "Long enough to learn and pass on the information. Not so long that your corruption can stand. It's that or just burn down each department every once in a while and start over. Buy some device from the Guild that can detect corrupt cops and publish the results of every interview so the bad ones can't protect their friends."

"I can see why you weren't popular with the folks back at the office," her voice had a mirthful, teasing edge now. "When did you become such a cynical bastard?"

"One of my previous lifetimes," his grin grew wider. "Working off all that karma by trying to remember that the point of police is to protect the world from predators, not to become the predators that protect politicians. People forget that. It's why the world sucks so much."

"Can it be salvaged?" she asked, eyes growing more serious now.

He shrugged and drank some coffee as he watched that cop get seated at a table across the way. They both listened to another man at a nearby table trying to explain the bond market troubles to someone on a cell phone.

"I have to try, Rachel," Greyson finally said. "If I can't make the city a better place, why the hell am I wearing this badge? Why are you? Why are any of us, if the alternative just makes us a better-placed gang than any of the others?"

"Is the whole Bureau made up of bad apples?" she asked in a tiny voice.

"I'm hoping that there's at least one honest cop left," he fixed his gaze upon her and let the implications color her face a pretty pink.

Silence engulfed them like a flash flood running down the canyon. Greyson pulled at the stack of papers, making almost a production of flipping to a point about halfway deep until he found the right date.

He didn't know why it was the right date, but he did. Five days before Kelly Anne had seduced and killed Carlos Dominguez. Greyson flipped a couple of pages slowly before he found the one he wanted. A day when a man was reported missing by his girlfriend when he didn't come home from work one night.

Valdis Pandev. Baltic immigrant. Pain in the ass that had been arrested a few times, but never had anything stick.

Contacted the police three days later with a cock and bull story about a huge fight with his girlfriend that had caused him to move out and never go back. Police had marked the case closed at that point, without telling the woman.

End of story.

That was one of the reasons he had made Rachel run a full query, without filtering it in any way. Open cases wouldn't have shown this bastard, and Greyson didn't want to tell others what he was looking for. What subtle cues might lead him to his killer.

Got to preserve that mystique of being a hunter. He could filter the whole stack of names down fast enough.

Greyson checked the vital information again. Delivery driver for one of the local networks, like a taxi service for food. Disappeared and returned from the dead three days later like Jesus risen.

Blond hair. Strong jaw. Pretty blue eyes. List of tattoos on arms, legs, and back, but nothing visible when the man wore pants and long-sleeves.

Greyson had a pretty good idea the man could squat for hours without any pain. You had to learn that trick in a Russian prison, where there were too many people sharing too small a space without benches, and frequently piss running on the floor because the jailers didn't care that much about cleaning things.

He'd be happy to apologize to the man if Valdis didn't end up being Siberian Mafia, but Greyson doubted that the odds were stacked too far against them on this one.

"Is that him?" Rachel asked quietly, eyes looking but no part of her body reacting.

Greyson started a bit internally, remembering that he had company and an audience today. Too many breakfasts in this joint alone with his thoughts, he occasionally forgot that the rest of the human species existed as more than obstacles on the sidewalk and noise machines to ignore.

"Working theory," Greyson replied, carefully flipping to the next page as an excuse to mislead anyone else watching.

"How do you do that?" she asked, hiding her mouth behind the coffee mug as she went for another sip.

"Cop magic," Greyson grinned sideways.

He couldn't explain it any better than that. Nor could the Army recruiters who had pulled him out of Advanced

Training and offered him something better than a rifleman's job. The folks at the police academy had made calls before he even emerged from the far end with his certification, and Greyson had walked right into Hunter Training when everyone else was just learning how to walk a beat.

Ethen nodded. Still waters that were deep enough to drown even a Phrenic. He'd been ordered to become Greyson Leigh as an insurance policy against the cops finding anyone else good enough to hunt Zaborra with Dominguez no longer an option. He certainly wasn't supposed to fall in love with the man and want to live with him.

As him, if he could.

If Greyson Leigh could even be corralled by a Phrenic infiltrator, and not take them both Deathwalker at some point.

More pictures. More names. More lives lost, but as far as Ethen knew, Zaborra was still happy with that Lithuanian bastard, although he hadn't checked in for more than a week as he went deep cover. Zaborra might have just gotten bored and gone shopping for more suits to wear.

Fucker was like that.

Greyson finally found Kelly's picture. Reread the bits her roommate had put into the system when the flouncy blond didn't come home or go to work for a few days. About the same time Carlos Dominguez got what he might have had coming, depending on how kind and loving God really was.

Mean streets of Boston didn't put Greyson into a particularly religious frame of mind. Unless Satan had already won. There was always that.

"So how do I absorb your cop magic, Greyson?" Rachel asked. "Short of being a Phrenic myself and sucking your damned brains out of your eye sockets."

He had another jolt of déjà vu so hard that he nearly spilled his coffee.

"Hey, you okay?" she asked, face turning concerned.

Greyson remembered to breathe.

"Sorry, bad image went too deep," he offered weakly. "That was why she killed Carlos. To be able to get inside the investigation and derail it."

Another deep breath.

The waitress saved him by returning with plates: ham, eggs, browns, and bread; and then immediately refilling coffee with a smile, as if she had decided maybe this was a date after all and he and Rachel were working things out.

"You don't learn cop magic," Greyson finally said around a bite of English muffin. "You're born with it. Hunters are, at least. They saw the spark inside you when you came along. The key is to understand that you have it, and then learn to harness it, like saddling a horse so you can ride it. From there, my job is to show you how to bubble it up from your subconscious into a tool you can hold in your hand. Things like standing in that apartment and looking inside their oven and their fridge. Asking odd questions because something just doesn't sound right at the surface. Like: who could walk up to her door without anybody noticing?"

"Eye of newt, toe of frog?" Rachel asked around her eggs.

"More truth than lies, Asher," he replied.

Because he was in true danger of making a mess, Greyson put his fork down and carefully picked up the two stacks of paper, tapping it with one definitive finger in front of Rachel, God, and everyone else in here like he had found the person he wanted, and then slid the two stacks together, with the older stuff on the bottom and a set of nobodies on the page up.

Rather than stuff them back into their envelope like a smart cop, he just shifted the entire stack over to the far corner from where it had been, out of the way but open to whoever *just happened to walk by.*

If they understood what they were looking at.

At no point had he looked at the cop across the way longer than enough to fix a description in his mind for later. Didn't mean he wasn't tracking the man when the guy stood up not long after that and made his leisurely way to the restrooms in back. Greyson studiously focused his eyes on Rachel as soon as he saw the man move.

Peripheral vision was a lovely thing to develop.

The Army had taught him to shovel the food in like they would take the plate away after an unknown number of seconds, so he was done before Rachel was. Pulled out his handheld and checked messages and updates with his head down.

"Let me know when he comes back out," Greyson muttered quietly under the noise of the other folks eating and chatting.

She took that as a cue and ate faster. Greyson felt a tap on his shin from her foot and saw her glance his way. He nodded minutely and went back to what he was reading in the latest issue of the Economist.

Every week, somebody interesting died and got the obit page. Those were always wildly interesting bits of history to learn.

A shadow loomed ever so briefly as Greyson nodded to some internal beat, and then it was gone.

"Are all narcs that obvious about it?" she muttered under her breath a few moments later.

Greyson looked up at her and put his handheld away.

"Hey, you're too dense to realize you've had a tail all morning," he said with a serious face. "And I'm a washed up has-been who shouldn't be left alone with a gun, you know."

The grin was back in her eyes.

"Cop magic," she murmured.

"You got it, young lady," he said. "They're going to madly

race off to look up poor Herbert Lam and think that they've stolen a march on us."

"Because he happened to be the random second person on the random page you left the stack open to," she said. "After making a production of pointing him out to the rookie who doesn't understand anything about how you big, bad detectives work?"

Greyson just smiled at her.

"Narcs are where you end up when Vice is too much to handle," he said with a hint of a sneer to his voice. "To say nothing of ever making it to Homicide Detective."

"You are a bad man, Greyson Leigh," she shook her head just a little, implying an eyeroll without actually committing one.

"Wait until you see what I'm like if they piss me off, Rachel," he replied.

[13]

HUNTERS

GREYSON KNEW HE COULDN'T RELY ON THE COMPUTERS at the station at this point. Every query would be logged automatically by the AI systems. Normally, that wasn't a problem, but today that meant that someone else would most likely be following the investigation in almost real time if he was dumb enough to let them.

Maybe they thought he was. Greyson decided to play a joke on someone as they emerged from breakfast, ignored the Scout across the parking lot as they climbed into the Jouster.

"Okay, rookie," he looked over as his seat belt snapped into place, chuckling as Rachel was having issues. Something about breasts, neck ties, and seat belts not wanting to cooperate this morning. "You call the station and have them run as much as they can find on Herbert Lam for us, to be printed and picked up later."

"Why printed instead of just being sent to the handhelds or the unit in the car?" she asked, finally getting all the painful bits straightened out. "Seems less efficient."

"Oh, it is," he assured her. "But stuff on paper has a solidity that can't be edited later."

123

As she started the car, he put a hand on her arm and his other finger to his mouth for silence, tapping the microphone on the radio comm in the dash.

Chandler Jouster only looked a little like this internally, while the outside was a near flawless match. The government Skycruiser in disguise had several other sets of systems added in later. The Guild-supplied lift system that seemed to use something like anti-gravity to move the car in three dimensions when you needed speed and maneuverability. But that Buck Rogers stuff was mixed here with a radio unit at least as old as Greyson in design, if not more. Electricity, crystals, and antennae that let you talk to people miles away as if by magic to someone born in the Nineteenth Century.

At least it had been magic until the aliens had brought down real magic, or at least a technological equivalent thereof.

Rachel nodded as she understood. Every police car was keyed to the same set of teeth, so any cop's keys could get into any other car in an emergency and drive it off without having to find the officer who had driven it before.

Made things better in a chase or getting someone to the hospital in a pinch, but it also meant that the Vice cop's partner could have easily climbed into Rachel's car and done things while everyone else was eating.

Worse, Greyson couldn't find whatever it was and suppress it without letting them know that he'd seen them, so they had to act casual for now. Rachel was out in the street, driving with the folks running late to work, so traffic was on the back side of stupid right now.

"We're going to need to do a lot of poking and walking today," Greyson announced for her and the others. "Let's find a place to park on the north side and we'll go from there until we're done and can come back for your wheels."

Rachel eyed him sharply sidelong, but nodded.

"Parking ticket or cheap lot?" was all she asked.

"Cheap lot," Greyson replied. "It is a bad habit to get into, to just be able to blow off and fix parking tickets because you have a badge and a gun."

Again, the faintest hint of pink coming up her cheeks, like maybe Rachel Asher hadn't always been a good cop, and was still discovering that she had some bad habits to undo. Carlos Dominguez hadn't been even close to the best role model, as far as Greyson was concerned.

As long as it didn't cost him his prey, Greyson was okay taking her the long way around to turning her into a good cop, and a better one.

Greyson nodded. Lesson learned, without him having to beat her about the head with a three-days-rotting sand shark to do it. Not that he disliked Icelandic cuisine, but there were some smells you'd never get out of your coat after you spilled some.

They found a parking lot not that long a walk from Boston Common. Tourist season was over for now, and winter tourism wasn't running, so they managed to squeeze the big, steel-colored beast in and emerged into the mid-morning sun on foot, two tourists in brown longcoats that didn't fit in with the moms or *au pairs* hauling the kids around the park.

The air had a hint of crispness to it, to go with the huge drifts of brown, crunchy leaves the city hadn't gotten picked up or mulched down yet. The trees were artistically nude today, rather than that dirty edge of nakedness you got in cheap pornography.

Fall had been a little dry other than the last few days, and the city was too cheap to water, so the grass was patchy brown already. They stayed mostly on the sidewalks though, passing strollers and vendor carts hawking pastries and coffee, plus one ambitious old weirdo with tattoos and a shaved head, dressed like a fireman and playing bagpipes for the busking bucket at his feet.

Greyson threw a twoonie coin in there as they walked by just because anybody willing to let his freak flag fly that boldly deserved a little support.

Greyson stopped at a stand on wheels to order a coffee he would throw away later, mostly still full, just as a way to stand around and watch who was following them right now. The Common landscaping made it a pain in the ass to hide when tailing someone, unless you had a big enough group to have one team in the car just circling outside, while others followed on foot at a safe enough distance.

This must be the partner, Greyson decided as he watched another man in a cheap gray suit intently studying a pile of dead leaves in the middle distance. Big fellow. Anglo like Greyson, but starting to lap over his belt as the pot belly got up a head of steam. Shaved head that still showed a shadow of a brown ring above the ears.

He never had understood why cops did that. Sure, they all assured themselves that it made them look tough, but it also advertised a set of self-image neuroses that Greyson found a little pathetic, like an older woman getting bad plastic surgery on her face and breasts, and forgetting what her hands and neck looked like.

Didn't help that both of his grandfathers still had full heads of white hair, as did his dad. Maybe he could afford that little bit of vanity. But a cop with a paunch and a shaved head just smelled like a bully to him, even from this distance.

They had paid and started walking again.

"We're not drinking this, are we?" Rachel asked after taking a tentative sip.

Greyson wanted to turn and look at the cop back there, just to see if he was talking into a cufflink, but figured he could stretch this game out all day if he was patient. And he needed the entertainment. Something about hunting had awakened a bit of his soul that had thought it was gone forever.

"We are not," Greyson acknowledged as he took just enough of a sip to confirm how bad Carl's coffee still was.

That man had long since decided that the dark roasts of the big, national chains just weren't burned anywhere close to enough, so he had to top it. In layman's terms, Greyson liked his coffee about a two. The three big chains generally went in for about a four or five, depending.

Carl thought six was for wimps.

But Greyson never actually drank the stuff. Just used it as cover, because Carl liked to sit in the middle of the most open space he could find. Every bit of sun, wind, rain, or snow hit without any cover, so other vendors looked for more sheltered places, and that left Carl his own little monopoly in this part of the park. Pastries weren't bad, if you paid attention to expiration dates.

Carl cut corners there, too.

"So are we actually hunting today, or just torturing people?" Rachel lengthened her stride to keep up as Greyson started walking hard.

"Man can't do both, Rachel?" he asked innocently.

Too bad there weren't any glass storefronts he could use to watch their tail. Rachel Asher was probably in better shape than Greyson was. Cop back there would be huffing and cursing soon. And eating lunch out of a microwave in a convenience store, hoping he didn't drip anything on his tie, because Greyson was planning on not stopping movement for the rest of the day unless he lost these turds first.

Tail has to be ready to move at a moment's notice. Big breakfast meant that Greyson could skip lunch, or maybe buy an apple off a cart somewhere, all the while dragging his two tails by the leash until they got tired, pissy, and started keeping score on who owed them favors back at the station for all this hard work.

Greyson would have loved to be able to listen in on that conversation. To see who had sicced these two on him and Rachel. To know if it was Owens in charge, or if Zielinski just couldn't let it go.

Or some third player, which is probably what Upkins was looking for. Nail the obvious candidates down hard, and then set her fox loose to see who suddenly emerges from the brush chasing him.

Yeah, he could see Denise going that way.

Once they crossed outside of the Common, it was like walking on the surface of another planet, not that Greyson could ever admit to doing something like that to anyone without checking their security clearances first. Suddenly they were back in an overpopulated ant nest of people, hives reaching to the sky like middle fingers offering the gods political commentary disguised as architecture.

A lot of this neighborhood had been ripped down and rebuilt over the last generation, both before and after the aliens had arrived. Ground floor retail with doors on the outside and inside, onto an inner food and relaxation court you could use to escape the extremes of Boston weather. Mezzanine level shops above that, only accessible from the inside and cheaper by the square foot. Couple of nice restaurants around here he'd have to make sure Rachel was aware of.

The transition from light to dark was like entering a tunnel, which was part of the point. Greyson had picked a regular door instead of passing through the sandwich shop on the left or the donut joint on the right, both of which were well lit. Tossed his coffee into a trash bin without breaking stride and turned Rachel hard past the donut joint and up an open flight of stairs to the mezzanine above.

He was counting footsteps in his head with a malicious smile on his face. At the top of the stairs Rachel abandoned her coffee as well, and Greyson more or less dragged her by the arm into a used bookshop that didn't believe in overlighting things. Swore all that extra illumination did bad things to the books and the humans, so the place was partly gloom.

The owner was a semi-reformed accountant who had seen the light of day and turned herself into a goth. Too hard edged to be a hippy, but that had probably been the other option, assuming that being born again was going to be too mundane for someone like Liz.

They exchanged nods as Greyson hauled Rachel all the way to the back of the shop, where Liz had put up bookcases over the windows. Liz kept entire walls of romance books here, organized alphabetically by sub-genre rather than author. Said it paid off most of her bills every month, just turning that stock over to office drones in the nearby towers looking for a better escape than drudgery and retirement.

"Cop/alien porn?" Rachel asked in a whisper, running a finger down a spine and pulling it out to look at the back.

"Everybody's got a different kink," Greyson replied quietly, ignoring his partner to watch the front of the shop.

By now the tail should have made it inside the building, but he'd been hanging back too far, and lost them in the transition, so he should be frantically racing around, calling his partner, trying to see where they'd gone off to.

If the man was smart, he'd get elevation so he could see over the crowds on the first floor and sunken conversation and relaxation pits scattered around. That was part of the reason Greyson was in the back here, hiding behind Liz's spike-studded skirts, as it were.

Not that Greyson would ambush a fellow cop and put

the man in the hospital in an honest mistake. At least not today. Tomorrow might be a different conversation.

"Jesus, Leigh," Rachel's whisper caught his ear. "Some people need to get out more."

He glanced to see she'd opened the book and was reading a section about a third in.

Given the cover picture, he assumed that this one wasn't anything remotely like a sweet romance. Most likely down at the other end of the spectrum, where you needed to show ID in order to buy it in some jurisdictions.

Greyson shrugged. As long as consenting adults consented, it wasn't generally a crime, so he didn't care. Hell, fornication outside the bonds of holy matrimony was still a crime on the books in many places, regardless of how long it had been since anyone had actually been prosecuted.

If a human and an alien were compatible enough and willing…

There. The tail had finally caught a clue. Greyson froze, his face mostly hidden by a bookcase, as the cop stopped right outside the dark shop and turned his back this way, looking out over the mob below.

Sure enough, his handheld came up and angry tones went back and forth.

"Silence your phone," Greyson whispered to his partner, doing the same. "And ignore it when it rings."

She gave him an eyebrow, but did so immediately.

Ten seconds later her handheld buzzed with an incoming call. Greyson smiled as she blinked in surprise.

Cop out there looked around until Rachel's phone stopped vibrating. More angry words with whoever he was talking to, but they weren't clear enough to understand with the acoustics of the book store.

Bullethead finally snarled something rude, stuffed the handheld into his jacket and vanished.

"He's gone," Liz's voice rolled out of the ether after a bit. "Down the stairs and crossing straight out the other street entrance."

Greyson gestured with his head for Rachel to join him and went up front.

"Thanks, Liz," he said as he stopped at the counter, Rachel in tow.

"Not a problem," the woman smiled up at them from her seat. "Got cameras up on the façade so I could see what was up. Why are cops chasing you today, Leigh?"

Greyson shared the grin. Liz was somewhere on the far, soft side of sixty. White hair, white makeup, black lips, and black leather with strange designs on it. She'd had the place for at least the last ten years, occasionally filling in Greyson's book collection, and then later liquidating it when he downsized.

"Training day," he said. He gestured as Rachel joined them. "This is my new partner, Rachel Asher. Rachel, Liz Morgan, old friend."

Rachel still had that damned book in her hand as Liz rose and they shook.

"I thought you stopped being a cop, Greyson," Liz noted inquisitively as she sat again. "Had it with those gestapo thugs."

"Relief pitcher," he said vaguely, not wanting to drag her down into his troubles. "One last case, and training the kid, and then back to the old life."

Rachel had put the book down on the counter, and a couple of toonies with it. She looked up at him like she was making sure he noted she was paying for the book instead of asking a favor from a potential informant. Of course, paying for things was how you generated the kinds of goodwill that would cause people to call you with tidbits later.

"This is part of a whole series, dear," Liz said as she made change out of a shallow bowl. "Eighteen of them so far. The missing ones are over in the LGBTQ section, for obvious reasons."

"Starting with one," Rachel said as she pocketed her change and stuffed the book in her outside left longcoat pouch. "Not sure how soon I'll have the time to actually read it, with Greyson holding final exams this week."

"You won't find a better professor, girl," Liz smiled. "And your friend just went back out the far door, after coming back in and looking around for ten seconds on the off-chance you thought he was gone and would step from cover."

Greyson watched Rachel lean over the counter to see the four screens back there, one of which was a feed from her handheld with the news, and three that were security cameras inside and outside for shoplifters and trouble.

"I don't like things sneaking up on me, Constable," Liz grinned.

"Good to know," Rachel nodded, turning his direction. "Next stop?"

"Tailor first, and then we're going to see a man about a horse."

[14]

A MAN AND A HORSE

Greyson had amused himself by taking Rachel to see Dominic the tailor and slipping the man twenty Canadian, a sammie for the salmon on the front of the coin, to spend an hour updating Greyson's measurements on file and then measuring her like she was going to order her own suit in the style of one of those fancy ones Dominguez had filled his closet with once upon a time.

All the while, Dominic had kept up a running commentary on cut, bias, fabric, drape, silhouette, etc. The little things that a cop who wanted to know fashionable clothing needed to understand. At least well enough to write down good observations and then come to this tiny little cave at the back of an ancient red brick block converted to shops.

Dominic had accidentally solved more than one case for him, just by asking those little questions about a man's suit that probably screamed like fire truck sirens to the ancient man when Greyson described them.

We all have an expertise that makes us valuable. The key

for Greyson lay in identifying each person's superpower and remembering it against need later.

"Now what?" Rachel asked as they emerged back into the mid-afternoon sun. "A man with a horse, you said earlier?"

Greyson looked both ways as they hit the sidewalk, but didn't see the goobers from this morning. Didn't mean they weren't around, just not visible. Maybe he'd gotten lucky and lost them for good. At least until Rachel went back for her car later, on the way to the station.

Hopefully, those boys would be angry enough to do something stupid at some point. Hunters didn't pull rank very often, because most cops were smart enough to leave them alone. Wasn't the same as not trying.

He could always let Denise have them. She'd probably enjoy that part.

"Now we go talk to a man about a horse, yes," Greyson replied, flipping his collar up.

The sun was starting to disappear into a hazy overhead, and the temperature was right at the bottom edge of comfortable. Should have dressed warmer, but Greyson still didn't trust Weather Control to get it right. At least most of the rest of this would be indoors.

Greyson led her to the nearest bus stop and waited, checking arrival times and destinations on his handheld with a wry grin. Public transit above ground still sucked in this town, unlike the centuries-old subway systems down in Gotham, but it was the perfect cover to avoid nosy cops.

Rachel stood beside him, eyeing a couple of punks who looked like they had planned on being annoying to the other riders. She could handle herself, but Greyson didn't need an official altercation, after all the effort he had gone through to disappear.

He pulled out his nifty new badge holder, flipped it open at them, and smiled.

"Ride another bus," he said curtly, leaving no doubt as to his intentions if these two punks got mouthy.

It was rude, and possibly unethical, ever so slightly, but he never claimed to not have a small soul. The next bus pulled up and Greyson waited until everyone else was aboard, leaving him with the two punks, before he got on and nodded at the driver.

She must have smelled cop, or maybe Rachel had flashed a badge, because the driver nodded back with a broad smile and turned back into traffic.

Rachel was standing midway back, one armed wrapped around a chrome pole for support.

"Valdis?" she asked quietly, mostly covered by the sounds of the wheezing machine and other passengers in their own worlds.

"This is the exact moment when everyone else would screw it up," Greyson replied, grabbing the pole as well and keeping it between them as a boundary. "We're playing a hunch, so we can't get remotely close to the man until we're ready to arrest him and drag the bastard back to the yard. Otherwise, he runs, disappears, and the killings go on."

"How does a…person vanish like he's done?" Rachel asked, not even voicing the name Phrenic in a public place where people might get nervous.

"He'll have a lair," Greyson leaned down closer, like he was whispering sweet nothings or dirty jokes in her ear.

She smelled nice. Something floral and natural, rather than an industrial chemical trying too hard. Vanilla and roses, maybe. Must be what she washed that brown hair in.

The woman didn't bother with makeup. She still had the bloom of youth on her features, when she wasn't scowling.

"Lair?"

Greyson brought himself back to Earth.

"Most likely something underground," he replied. "In

past cases, they took their kills back there like a squirrel with their nuts, hiding them in a tree. Have you ever seen a body they killed?"

"Only Dominguez."

"That doesn't count," he said. "He was only just dead. When they have time, they drain the body like a spider. You get a really light mummy, just bones and skin. They can still pull enough material out to change, so once one of these killers gets set up, he'll keep a handful of bodies there. Lets him go back and forth between shapes. Fortunately, they can only change to a new form while tasting someone, except for when they revert to base model with the scutes."

"Where would he hide them?" Rachel's eyes got bigger, then narrower, like the anger had welled up and pushed the astonishment to one side.

"My guess is someplace mostly abandoned," Greyson offered. "Lot of old steam tunnels and such under a city like this. Not all of them are in use. If Valdis is our killer, finding that's going to be hard, because he moves around a lot."

"What about his car?" Rachel asked. "Where's it?"

Greyson thought she had punched him in the nose, from the way his head jolted back.

Shit, I've grown old and lazy. Been thinking too much about the man and not the disguise.

Phrenic exists in a social matrix. Use it, dummy!

Ethen nodded sagely, He hadn't thought of that, either.

Greyson smiled at Rachel after a moment.

"See, you've already learned the best lesson I can teach you," he murmured into her hair. "Ask the weird questions. Forgot about that car for now, but we'll ask the system to spit out a current or recent location after we talk to his boss."

"It's safe, walking into the boss's office?" Rachel's face got confused.

"I'm not asking polite questions when we get there, Rachel," Greyson felt his smile turn hard and cold. "We're both bad cops and he's potentially got a serial killer on staff. If he says anything that spooks Valdis, the man gets brought up on felony charges and then probably put in jail. Hunters have a lot of case law on their sides for exactly this reason."

"And those two dipshits from Vice would dance around the serious questions while asking just enough to warn the man, who in turn says something to Valdis and blows it all up."

She nodded. Greyson did as well.

"Seen it happen too many times before," he said, popping his neck as an excuse to stop smelling her hair.

This woman was young enough to be his daughter. He didn't need to remember that she was female. She was a cop and that was that.

"Double bad cop?" she smiled up at him.

"Training day, rookie," he scowled. "You use anger as a shiv, not a hammer. Gets better results if the target is still around to watch himself bleed out, rather than being out cold on the floor."

Three bus transfers later, Greyson found himself standing in front of a decrepit office building, faded mustard paint done in concrete ugly, on the edge of a warehouse district. Sun was just about an hour from the horizon, back there behind the growing clouds, and the temperature was steadily falling.

He'd need some good coffee after this interview, just to stay warm, and to brace himself against the coming stupidity when he got back to Headquarters later.

"That's it?" she asked, almost disappointed.

"Most of it exists up in the datastream," he replied. "One reasonably powerful computer as a traffic cop routing information around. Someone like Nazarian opens her handheld and places an order by pushing some buttons in an app. The restaurant gets the order and the money and starts cooking. A driver gets a signal to pick it up for delivery and an address. He gets paid when Kelly marks the delivery complete. The guy we're talking to doesn't do much more than handle complaint calls from drivers and customers, making sure he's got enough people on call for the late day surge and for the midnight munchies. For all that he gets a percentage."

"You've done this before?" she asked.

"Everybody has been too tired or lazy to cook at some point," he grinned. "Most people haven't ever wondered at the plumbing underneath and gone looking. But I've never had to run a case through someone like this. Surprised, actually, when I think about it, but I suppose there are too many records, too much data, for a normal criminal to evade capture for long. Our boy doesn't really care, because he's not Valdis and can go be someone else if the cops show up."

They went into a lobby. Greyson checked the listing board while trying to identify the smell. Rotting kimchi left in the sun until it was almost dry had a similar aroma. Covered over with enough ammonia to make a skunk sneeze.

He'd been through worse.

Up the stairs for the exercise, and not because he didn't want to get stuck in the small box when it inevitably broke down. Rachel followed, hopefully learning better habits.

Third floor. Turn right. Fourth door. KG Services, Inc.

Greyson tried the handle, but it was locked.

He rang the buzzer instead.

"Go away," an angry voice emerged from a speaker. "Not interested in Salvation and I'm not buying anything."

Greyson glanced over at Rachel in a nearly matching

outfit to his: brown pants, nice shirt, darker brown longcoat, her in a tie; and wondered what sort of idolaters had emerged from the masses that they dressed like cops.

She smiled back, as if asking the same question.

Greyson flipped open his badge and held it up for the camera lens on the buzzer.

"I can always come back with a warrant and kick your fucking door in," he said in a casual voice. "Your choice."

Somehow, he was not surprised that the lock buzzed a moment later.

Rachel pushed the door in and he followed.

Small office without a bathroom. Probably a locked one down the hall somewhere. Desk, two chairs, stained green couch that looked older than Rachel was. Not quite Greyson's age. Bad landscape art on the walls. Half-high refrigerator behind the desk. File cabinet four drawers high. Server tower rack atop the fridge, with two processing blades in it humming quietly.

Man behind the desk was a pudgy middle age with a white-boy-fro receding from a fivehead. Skin like a dead fish in its paleness. Hadn't showered today, but maybe in the last week or so.

Little tray on the desk, almost buried in papers, had a pair of incense sticks furiously fighting a losing battle with entropy and smell. Screen on the desk facing the other direction so Greyson couldn't tell what was on it, plus a keyboard and a light pen, both resting right now like tired birds.

Greyson noticed a headset with a red light in one ear, so not in the middle of a call.

"Make it fast?" the man asked in a nasally-high voice. "Rush hour going on right now and I got all the usual idiots complaining that the driver's two minutes late."

Greyson walked right over to the chair and sat down, showing the man his badge again. Rachel remained a step to one side, like maybe the moron would try to run from them and had to get past her. If so, he'd have been better off bringing the entire Bolivian army first.

"Looking for one of your drivers," Greyson smiled.

"Not mine, pal," the man snapped. "Independent contractors on 1099's. Got the best lawyers and accountants in town handling that side of things."

"Noted." Greyson decided he could try the agreeable approach first.

Rachel could always flip the man face down on the desk with an arm bar if that was what it took to get cooperation.

"I want to know if he's working tonight, and what zones he normally runs in," Greyson said.

"Got a warrant?"

"Do I need to take your whole fucking life apart first, just to get an answer?" Greyson smiled. "Shut you down for the three days before I am constitutionally required to let you post bail? That is, assuming a forensic pass through your systems proves to be utterly spotless and I can let you restore your hardware from a recent backup because I've wiped the systems seven ways while digging?"

Greyson loved that element of fear that crept into the man's eyes.

Personally, he didn't know anything more about computer systems than he did cars, but he had dated a nerd once, after Denise and before Emmy. Learned that they're just as bad at being gearheads as car people, and that you can learn a stupid amount of jargon by just listening when she wants to rant over a glass of wine. That's generally all a woman ever wants, is to be listened to and believed. Good ones don't need you trying to solve the world. They usually need cuddling, too, but that fell at a different point in the evening.

Greyson watched the man stew. Amazingly, he didn't need to walk the two of them through the Kubler-Ross personally, as the man got himself past anger and on to acceptance without any untoward activities on Rachel's part.

"Name?" he asked in a tired voice, already exhausted by the mental effort of being nice, probably.

"Trade me places and I'll look him up," Greyson stood abruptly. "That way, you can't be held as an accomplice later, if the man suddenly flees from justice tonight."

More fear.

Bad cop didn't always mean screaming. Sometimes the threats were so subtle that they slid in between your ribs almost politely.

Like reminding the man he could still be in cuffs and a Black Maria van if Greyson felt like getting ugly.

More ugly.

Rachel growled.

It took everything Greyson had not to goggle at her when she did, but the man behind the desk did that enough for both of them. He came out of that seat like an ejector was clearing him during a failed rocket launch.

"You sit here," she pointed, sounding like Nemesis herself come down to referee today's match.

Greyson waited until the victim did, and then walked around to the other side.

As he suspected, pretty simple system. Didn't do much more than forward messages and do best-time calculations to locate drivers. Greyson found the menu item he wanted, called up Valdis Pandev, and located his most recent stop. That boy had already been busy tonight.

Greyson and Ethen both wondered if perhaps the man

smelled the walls closing in and was looking for an escape route.

Valdis/Zaborra didn't have much time left.

Next, Greyson looked up patterns, noting that their prey generally preferred to stay in only seventeen zones, a compact footprint that included downtown and generally stayed south of the river.

Something about the image triggered a vision in Greyson's mind. An old business campus that had steam tunnels from when it had been all part of a larger conglomerate. He could not rid himself of the image.

Quickly, Greyson reset the system to the basics and stood.

"Thank you," he offered the fuming man. "Painless. Don't go looking in your log files to see who I was tracking and we'll be fine. If anything goes wrong with my investigation, even the off-world colonies will honor any extradition request I might choose to file, so you'll never get away from me."

The man wanted to snarl, but thought better of it.

Wise choice.

Greyson smiled and made his way past Rachel to the door. They did a complicated dance that ended up with Rachel in the hall, and the man back behind his desk.

Eight minutes had elapsed since the door had opened.

They emerged into twilight.

"You found something," she said quietly as they started to walk. "We don't need his car's current location, do we?"

"No," Greyson said. "But it was still a brilliant idea on your part. I do want to track it back a few days, because I might have just found his lair."

"Oh, shit," she said. "Do we call in heavy firepower?"

"He's not there," Greyson pointed out. "Just dropped some Chinese at a tower downtown for some working stiffs pulling an all-nighter. And if we try to hide a team that big, he'll probably notice something and flee. I need to make some calls, and then we'll avoid the office entirely."

"Because we're going hunting," Rachel nodded, reaching up under her jacket to touch the handle of her nerve scrambler.

"We are."

Greyson found them a quiet place to eat dinner and asked for a table as far away from everybody as he could get, flashing his badge so they understood the kind of privacy a cop might want.

He always carried cash in his pocket for the same reason. Nobody could really track your life by looking at your debit card in real time when cotton-plastic bills and silver coins changed hands. He and Rachel ended up back in a section that was currently closed off, away from regular people.

He dialed as soon as the waiter took their orders and left.

"Wondered who I'd hear from first," Edgar Redhawk said as he answered. "Everything okay with Rachel?"

"She's fine," Greyson replied. "Came clean eventually and I'm hoping you have a new boss so my case isn't blown."

"She's here in my office," Redhawk said. "Should I put you on speaker?"

"Please do," Greyson waited for a moment until the sound quality changed. "Denise, how close are you following things?"

"Couple of north end detectives have been sticking fresh

pins in their Greyson Leigh voodoo dolls today," *Her Honor* chuckled throatily.

"Anyone else in the room right now?" he asked simply.

"No, and we're currently clean," she replied. "Probably won't be tomorrow, but it's an ongoing battle."

"Rachel and I are playing a hunch," Greyson said. "In six hours, if I'm right, this case will be closed."

"And you aren't going to tell me anything, are you, Greyson?" Denise asked.

"If I did, it would leak," he sounded as apologetic as he could get. "One of you would feel compelled to put a team on backup, and if they knew what neighborhood I went hunting, they'd want to be close enough to help. Or would mention it to someone."

"And if he kills you?" Denise's voice picked up just enough emotion to let him hear it. "Then what?"

"I'll program a message with all the details for a 9AM delivery to the two of you," Greyson offered. "If it arrives, then Rachel and I are probably either dead or captured, which is the same thing and you'll need to have the Guild scan us if one of us walks into your office without the other."

"This wasn't what I had in mind when I called you back, Greyson," Denise's weathervane was leaning towards angry now, from the hints of wistful earlier.

"You knew who I was, Denise," he countered. "The scorpion and the turtle. Nothing's changed, except now you have a whole new raft of signals intelligence you can follow up on. Be interesting to see where it leads."

"Right now, to suspensions pending firing, Leigh," Redhawk spoke up. "Internal Affairs has instructions to make examples of those boys, if something can be made to stick, and I'm sure it can, so maybe prosecution after that."

"And they'll roll to save their hides and give you the next person up their chain," Greyson nodded as he listened.

Rachel watched him, watched the room, and looked like she was doing her best to not fidget at being left out of this poignantly-dangerous conversation. Even with as much as she might learn about how to play hardball with other cops.

At least she had this side of the conversation.

"That's the current theory," Denise spoke up. "As you surmised, Edgar has decided to look out for himself for once, instead of falling on his sword for a boss that was all set to throw him under a bus. There will be changes coming to the Bureau, and many of the local divisions. It's amazing what you can do when someone hands you a big enough hammer."

"Not every problem is going to be a nail, Metropolitan Upkins," Greyson observed dryly. "Keep your shiv in mind, too."

"Oh, it's always handy, Greyson," she smiled with her voice. "But I'll have a team on standby anyway. I can call some boys up from the District right now and have them orbiting and ready to drop without anyone on the ground knowing any better."

"Just give me radio silence, Denise," Greyson couldn't help the edge of threat in his voice. Even with her. "Odds are very good that tomorrow morning the case is done, one way or the other, and you'll have to decide what to do with me then."

"You still refuse to be a Captain, Leigh?" she asked.

"Without hesitation, Upkins," he growled.

"Then when you and your partner walk in tomorrow, we'll have a chat, just the four of us," *Her Honor* said simply.

"What else can I help you with, Leigh?" Redhawk asked.

Greyson gave him the information on the car and asked for a dump of all the times it had been tagged in the last two months by a surveillance camera, a red-light system, or a cop driving through parking lots looking for stolen cars.

"Not owned by Herbert Lam," Redhawk chuckled as Greyson heard him typing in the background.

"Red herrings are salty booby-traps, Redhawk," Greyson replied dryly. "You'd think cops would know better."

"You'd think," Edgar agreed. "Got the list, want it printed?"

"Absolutely not," Greyson almost snarled. "Dump it into a spreadsheet and send it to Rachel and I electronically. We'll do the crunching at this end."

"On the way," he said after a moment. "Anything else?"

"Prayers to Tyche?" Greyson asked. "Rachel and I are probably going to need the Goddess of Luck on our side tonight."

MAPS AND LIES

Greyson's humor at this point had been ground down to a fine, killing edge, so he told Rachel to pick up her car and drive it home, and then catch a bus or cab to his place.

And to dress for a cold night, but in layers she could remove later.

His memory said that those tunnels were warm.

He really didn't care if Rachel's tails managed to follow her to his apartment. Likely, they'd be so stupid that they expected the two of them to be fucking, rather than solving a case. But if they'd been any good as cops, Denise would have left him alone with his life.

Greyson had gone out once, to get the synth whiskey bottle refilled and pick up some dried fruit and jerky, just so he wasn't hunting on an empty stomach later.

Anything heavier would have soured him anyway.

By the time there was a knock at his door, Greyson had already converted the various coordinates Redhawk had sent into a map. All seventeen zones were bright with stars. Other places looked like trips to specialty stores for things that couldn't be delivered to an underground lair without a lot of questions.

Just because, he answered the door with the nerve scrambler in his hand. Emmy would understand that he was working, and anybody but Rachel might need to be turned into fresh chum for a shark.

"Pretty sure I got made," Rachel whispered as she slipped by him into the apartment.

Just because, he looked both ways out the door, but they were alone. Greyson set all of the locks and joined her in the kitchen area.

All the curtains were closed, so nobody could see in, but he had left both lamps on. His window probably looked like a bright yellow spot from the street.

As intended.

"Synth whiskey?" he asked, picking up his own glass and having a sip. "Good for the nerves and we'll be a little while before we can leave."

"Sure," she said, stripping off her jacket and laying it across the back of the couch.

She'd never been here, and the place didn't have many homey touches. Just furniture and the Murphy bed, currently up with the table down and a larger tablet than his handheld on it. A little art. One bookcase of things he still didn't want to part with yet.

Greyson filled a second highball with a finger and handed it to her.

Rachel had done her brown hair up into a braid, instead of leaving it down like she had all day. Probably anticipating combat and wanted it out of her way and her eyes if she had to shoot something.

Likewise, the nice slacks and shirt had given way to something that looked like army combat gear, in an appropriate speckled gray pattern, with boots instead of loafers. No tie tonight. Her longcoat was the only thing she had on from earlier, other than the shoulder holster with the nerve scrambler.

The semi-tight outfit framed her form and muscles. Five foot two, curvy, and tougher than most of the men on the force by a ways. Smarter than them, too.

Her face was cold and hard.

"What aren't you telling me?" Rachel asked as she took a sip.

Greyson had a moment of something other than déjà vu, but wasn't sure what to call it.

Had this conversation before, maybe?

He flashed back to another woman, a conversation that probably took place about the same time Rachel was busy being born.

The things he couldn't tell her, either.

"More than you probably imagine," as a peace offering. "More than I can even put into words, Asher."

"Cop magic?"

She was both serious and sarcastic now.

"Some of it, yes," he agreed.

The nightmares. The visions. The bizarre déjà vu moments over the last few days. None of that he could tell her, without even really being sure why, other than it would make her an enemy that might decide to kill him.

Ethen nodded, his hands hovering over the controls to stop Greyson Leigh from a true cop magic moment that suddenly made him understand why he knew so much about a Phrenic infiltrator, and this one in particular.

"So now what?" Rachel asked, glancing around the tiny space with a critical eye.

"Now we review the map," Greyson replied. "In a few minutes, we turn off one of the lights, and then the other a few minutes later, like we were necking on the couch first and then moved to the bed. Idiots outside might even fall for something so thin, and stop paying attention after about a half hour. That's when we leave. The building has an old tunnel that crosses under the street and we can exit over there, if they don't know about it."

"All this effort to get me to come back to your place?" she teased lightly. "You could have just asked."

Greyson shrugged. It wasn't like he didn't find her magnetic. Hard, athletic body. Hunter's mind.

If he'd been twenty-five years younger and single, he might have considered making a pass at the woman. But then, unlike Rachel, most women don't even start to get interesting until they passed thirty. At least in bed.

He grabbed the second chair and pulled it close without a word, sitting and bringing the tablet live.

"Messy," Rachel said as she sat and leaned her weight, her right breast, up against his arm to see the screen.

Twenty-five years younger and single.

"Watch," the cop in him came to the fore.

Greyson filtered for the last two weeks, instead of sixty days. Then he eliminated the hours of 4PM to 1AM. Working hours for a delivery driver.

"Oh, shit," she whispered so quietly someone sitting on the couch would have missed it.

"Yeah," Greyson glanced back at her. "You had a really good idea with tracking the car instead of relying on the driver. I would have gotten us close doing it my way."

"But this shows where he parks during the day," she completed the thought. "So the entrance to his lair has to be close."

"See these buildings?" Greyson asked, pointing to a cluster not far from the parking lot where Valdis left his car when he was sleeping.

"Yeah."

"Old corporate campus from thirty years ago," Greyson said. "Company went slowly bankrupt over the last ten, along with everyone else, and most of those buildings are abandoned these days. Electronic security systems in place at ground level, but not even guards watching. And there's a whole underground network that was built to let people stay out of the weather."

"How do you know about this place?" Rachel's weight shifted even closer, pressing herself more fully against his arm.

"Old case," Greyson hedged, unsure where the information came from, the visions so acute he could count the steps, other than he knew exactly what door Valdis was using. Where the man was stashing bodies. Where he slept.

Cop magic.

Rachel was breathing heavy. To someone on the outside it would probably sound like sexual arousal, and it was, in a way.

Hunter's High.

That moment when all the clues come together into a matrix, and all the fun bits of the brain light up with electrochemical rewards almost as potent as an orgasm.

Greyson had seen it before. And while she was a hot babe of a cop, he had no interest in taking advantage of his amazing new partner right now when she was in that state. Neither of them would probably forgive themselves for it later.

He stood abruptly and grabbed his glass, walking over and settling in the reading chair after turning it around far enough to watch her.

Rachel had a look of almost inconsolable disappointment on her face as she turned blankly and stared at him. Greyson took another sip of his synth whiskey and turned out the reading light.

Step One.

He watched her go through her own stages of something, even more happy that he was over here and not close enough for her to breathe on him. Or grab him.

After nearly a minute, she picked up her glass and walked to the living space part of the studio, eyes firmly locked on him as she did.

Greyson held up his glass as a silent toast. Watched her do the same. Finally, she settled on the near edge of the couch, still silent as the grave.

"So we're supposed to be necking right now?" she asked in a complicated voice. "As a prelude to you taking me to bed?"

"That's just the cover story I'm hoping those morons are telling each other right now," he countered. "Don't read anything into it."

She muttered something that his cop training wanted to lip read as *too bad*, but he didn't even let himself think about it.

Greyson took another sip and considered what he might do if she stood up right now, walked over, and climbed onto his lap like Emmy occasionally did. If her hair still smelled like vanilla and roses. What it might feel like if he were to run a hand through it and caught a handful at the end to tug.

Dreamers by evening, but he was a cop. They were hunters.

Maybe if Denise fired him tomorrow, he might consider something like that as a civilian.

Greyson watched Rachel's eyes finally return to normal. To the present tense.

He didn't want to know where she'd been. Wasn't ever going to ask.

She took a drink of the whiskey and started breathing normally again.

"Greyson…?"

"Don't fret about it, Rachel," he deflected her before they both ended up on thin ice again.

"Okay," she answered in a small voice. "What's a better way to kill time?"

The smile on her face was finally less serious. More back to the sarcastic Rachel he had just spent the day around.

The cop was finally back, and not the woman who walked into a white room to escape the job.

Rather than approach anything else, Greyson talked about the Phrenic, surprising himself with the wealth of detail he had accumulated over the years, from books, interviews, and even just an understanding of sentient beings and the Illymus Merchant Guild that had first brought humans the realization that they weren't alone in the universe. That there really were aliens out there.

A few minutes in, she reached up and turned out the light over her head, disappearing into a shadowed silhouette Greyson could watch against the back-lit curtains keeping the street at bay.

Worked better that way. With her dark skin and darker hair, she ceased being a person he wanted to seduce, and just became every cop ever, the rookie listening to the old man share nuggets of experience and luck disguised as wisdom.

So they talked in near darkness and encompassing silence. Nothing personal. Nothing random. Just aliens in general and Phrenic in particular. How to hunt them. How they hunted others. How to stop the next one that came along and tried to turn the Earth into their own, personal game preserve.

After almost an hour, Greyson was talked out. Everything

he knew on the subject had hopefully gotten filed away over there, and they could go kill this stupid bastard.

He stood and handed across her jacket before grabbing his own. Unlike her, he wasn't dressed in anything that might remind him of his commando days. No blacks. No knit cap. No war paint.

The past was done and dead, and they needed to look to the future. Ethen silently agreed, hoping that he could somehow survive the night as well.

Or if Zaborra would say something that caused Rachel to see Greyson/Ethen clearly enough to use a nerve scrambler on them.

At least if she did that, the truth would become clear fast enough. Greyson Leigh would revert to base form Ethen Boli.

As long as he got to kill Zaborra first, Ethen knew he'd be fine with that, coward or not.

He could never kill again. Never end a sentient life and suck out all their memories. Not after living inside Greyson.

Stealing the man and living out things as him was cheating, but there was nothing else Ethen could do to bring the man back. At least if he continued to be Greyson, he could help make the galaxy a better place, and turn Rachel Asher into the kind of cop that they made movies about.

Maybe that was the end of cowardice? Walking into something like this and not caring if you got killed, as long as it was for a higher purpose?

Ethen didn't used to be able to even spell introspection, but he would never escape the mind and mannerisms of Greyson Leigh, regardless of the future.

The best thing he could do now would be to honor the man as much as he could.

Greyson opened the door slowly, quietly, peeking out to see if anyone was there.

Clear, they emerged on silent feet. Because he always took the stairs, he led them to the elevator now. Got her pressed up against one side and him the other, invisible if the door opened midway.

Got them down to the laundry room unseen with any luck. Crossed under the street that hopefully had a pair of bored cops making rude conversation about partners. Maybe even Bullethead and his buddy, still on everybody's shit list after their failures today.

So far, so good.

Up a quiet flight of badly lit stairs and into the far side of the far lobby. Nobody around. Out the back onto an alley and stick close to the sides of the buildings, letting the trash dumpsters provide shelter as they moved.

Two ghosts stalking the nightwalkers.

[17]

INTO THE NIGHT

Greyson didn't own a car. Too much hassle and expense, so he had a budget for public transit and private taxis. He waited until they were four blocks away before he triggered the system to call for a ride.

If someone was watching his life that close, it wouldn't matter what evasions he tried. If not, they should be in the clear.

Just to be sure, he pulled Rachel into a recessed doorway for a closed shop and watched the street for watchers. They weren't snuggled up like lovers or even holding hands like a date. Just two people heading to a show, or home from dinner or something.

Twenty-five years younger and single. But he was never putting a tie on again either, even if Denise offered to keep him on staff.

The car showed and his handheld beeped to let him know. They climbed in to the sounds of steel drums and lost love wailing mournfully.

Sure, why not?

Carrib driver wanted to argue briefly about dropping

them off in the middle of nowhere. Probably afraid one of them was going to murder the other in the guise of a bad date or something, so Greyson showed the man his badge and that generated a wall of silence so thick and profound you could have walked across the river on it.

Rachel's badge just reinforced things.

Greyson spent a few minutes studying the driver out of the corner of his eye, wondering what the man might think he was guilty of. Everyone had that reaction to the badge, even legitimate citizens, so he could make up whatever story he wanted.

Put a smile on his face, wondering if the guy was kidnapping middle-aged stockbrokers and selling them into sexual slavery on a G'schtack colony somewhere, just because there was a kink for everything.

Or maybe the driver was secretly smuggling in alien kazoos and was going to undercut the Earth manufacturers and drive them out of business. Maybe he knew the secret for an advanced donut, and was driving nights to make enough capital to start his business?

The ride passed quickly and amiably.

"Why are you smiling?" Rachel finally asked as the driver waved once and lit out of there like all the hordes of hell were on his tail, leaving them alone in the middle of a mostly-abandoned parking lot.

So Greyson told her. Watched her face fall into blank shock even as his remained so humorous.

"Lemme guess," Greyson said. "All cop, all the time. Hard-nosed hard-ass who never relaxes and knocks one back with the boys after hours? That what they say about me?"

"Something like that, yeah," she breathed, furiously recalibrating things from the way her face moved.

"It's all true, Rachel," Greyson assured her. "Except the parts that aren't. And a few of them are fuzzy."

"So you're really just a dork in disguise?" she finally smiled again.

"In disguise?" his face almost hurt from the smile.

That got an eyeroll that made it all worthwhile.

Greyson serioused things by drawing his nerve scrambler and holding it low against his thigh. Out of view, but ready to fire.

The safety clicking seemed loud enough to wake the dead.

She didn't gulp or anything. Just drew her own and mirrored him. He supposed that growl earlier had been more like the Rachel Asher he should expect.

Competent. Lethal.

Invisible pixies led him across the parking lot to the parking space that seemed to be Valdis's favorite. Empty right now. Maybe reserved, since they had numbers in fading yellow paint.

Greyson flipped his collar up as the breeze started to bite. Moon had been out earlier but clouds had cast everything into shadow now. Jacket had a fancy seal the aliens had started selling people. Velcro without the noise or little bits of fluff that got stuck in them and had to be pried out with tweezers.

Felt like a night for a lid, but Greyson didn't do hats. Just not his thing. One would probably add character, but Hunters don't want to be memorable. Nothing that jars the memory if someone sees you later.

He rotated slowly in place, studying the rest of the parking lot, and the half-lit towers in the middle distance.

In his mind, he was almost another Phrenic hunting the first, in ways that he simply could not put words to. It felt awkward to walk as a human. The balance was wrong, the arms were a little too short, the eyes saw deeper into the purple and not as far into the red.

But he had stopped being anything but pure hunter now. Killer.

Rachel sensed it and fell into place on his wing as he started to walk, a pace back and a pace out on his left.

Mirrors.

There. A little depot to wait for a bus, maybe, except that it was also an entrance to the underground hallways. Greyson made a mental note not to shoot at movement. There might be a homeless person sleeping rough in there, although he doubted it, with the predators around. Maybe a rabbit or a possum, though.

Empty.

He reached into the pocket where he'd stashed his dried snacks and located the pocket flashlight he had tossed in there earlier.

Back to being a cop, with pockets full of magic items against need.

The space was about nine feet deep and twelve wide, with an overhang facing south to keep most of the weather patterns at bay. His light revealed the door on the back, hinged at the top to swing up and out of the way.

Somebody else's memory led Greyson to kneel at the center. Simple key lock in the middle of a horizontal handle holding the door closed, but it didn't look right.

The whole scene smelled wrong.

He put the nerve scrambler down and glanced over at Rachel, but she was all set to kill for him if something or someone jumped out. Greyson nodded and turned the handle.

It moved silently, like someone had removed the innards and left a hollow shell in place of the lock.

That sounded like a Phrenic way of thinking.

Greyson pushed the door and felt it move back and away from him. There were stairs down into the darkness, the mouth of the abyss itself yawing open to swallow his soul, except that whoever might want it was already too late for that.

He flashed the light down and revealed nothing but steps and a hallway disappearing in the direction of the towers.

A deep sigh of accomplishment felt appropriate. Everything until now had been pure speculation. The unlocked door meant a crime had occurred. Was occurring.

Awaited them.

Greyson picked up the nerve scrambler and stood gracefully. Rachel was armed, so he stuffed his into the holster for now and stepped down under the half-open hatch.

He nodded to Rachel and she joined him. Inside, Greyson closed the hatch and twisted the handle to spoof the lock closing.

It would never do for Valdis to get this close and smell a trap.

"Anybody likely to be down here?" Rachel murmured, watching the darkness with a flashlight she had attached underbarrel to her nerve scrambler.

Point. Shoot.

Greyson was suddenly in a Central American jungle again for a moment before he snapped himself hard back to the present tense.

"Anybody that would try their luck runs into a Phrenic, more likely than not," Greyson replied as he started down the steps. "That's only a problem once, so we'll assume we have the place to ourselves."

He checked his watch. Midnight.

Assuming Zaborra stayed true to schedule, he would be delivering for another hour or so, and then driving here to eat his own takeout meal and sleep.

Zaborra? No, Valdis.

Yes, Valdis.

Weird.

Down the stairs into the gullet of the galaxy's angriest whale.

The corridors down here had probably been sealed up when the corporation finally got too broke to afford the extra groundskeepers, as there wasn't much trash or graffiti. Kids had broken in a few times, but there were easier places to tag closer to bus stops, so the remoteness of this campus had actually protected it for the most part.

Greyson imagined the most that local cops had to worry about was folks steaming up windows of their cars in the parking lot behind him. As long as they kept their doors locked, he didn't imagine the other hunter would bother them. Too much effort, since he had a better gig right now.

Still, the déjà vu was so hard it was like he was riding on rails as he went up the hallway. After about one hundred feet, every third light fixture was working, throwing enough illumination he could put his light away.

Rachel still had a spotlight of death preceding her, but that was her choice.

Concrete floors and walls, like the builders had dropped in a rectangular sewer pipe in sections and then either cut out the spots they wanted to add lights, or skipped the full section and did a three-sided piece instead. He didn't care enough to go look up the architectural designs later.

Both of them walked in utter silence along a trail worn in the little bit of dust. Greyson could taste the stillness of the air, since there were no blowers down here to move it around. You would get heating and cooling cycles to push it back and forth a little, but that just meant the grit hung where you could chew it when you breathed through your mouth.

Not bad enough for a flu mask, but not all that pleasant.

Like being in a desert as the air finally settled from a sand storm.

Dream memory led him to a door. One of those access tunnels for Maintenance to do stuff behind the scenes, like a Hollywood set. He twisted the knob carefully, felt it give under his hand, so he nodded to Rachel and pushed it open.

Cop Magic. That was the story he would stick with. Déjà vu would likely get her to asking uncomfortable questions and she'd end up shooting him.

Not yet, little lady. You can kill me later, after we take Zaborra down. Not until then.

Greyson shook his head in confusion, unable to suppress the strange voices whispering in the back of his brain. They'd gotten worse over the last week, like precognition warning him that all this was coming, but that wasn't going to stop him from doing his job.

The room beyond was just another hallway, more or less. Wider in this section, where gardeners and cleaners could store gear. Nobody had ever bothered to steal a mop in a bucket, or a garden rake.

Greyson nodded as precognition held true and moved him deeper, glancing back occasionally to make sure his mirror image was still there. She'd get the kill, not him. He wasn't sure how he knew that, but somehow Greyson knew he'd freeze when it came time to shoot Valdis.

It would be like killing himself.

Farther in, back into the less pretty sections of the warren. Past a pair of long-dead bathrooms that had showers for the workers to clean up after their shift. No lights, so they had to rely on pocket flashes to see things, but the dust and grime in there, plus the spider webs, assured Greyson that his target wasn't here, or hiding things in this space.

Deeper.

They hadn't stored lawn mowing gear down here. The

company had always hired that out, and generally it was a group of Hispanic groundskeepers that would bring a flatbed trailer. Hardest working, most reliable folks on the planet, then or now.

But they could store other things in this basement. Salt for the winter snows. Spare fuel for the backpack blowers that screamed like *ban sidhes*. Parts. Whatever might be useful.

There was a door.

Satan himself awaited Greyson just on the other side of that barrier. He felt his heart start to finally pound with the mad energy of endgame.

The Hunt.

Thirty years later and his drill sergeant, the second one after he had been accepted into the killing corps, came back to him clear as yesterday.

Breathe deeply. Focus on the killing, and ignore everything else unless it impacts on your calculations for survival. Keep moving. Keep killing. They are more afraid of you are than you are of them.

The only fear you will acknowledge is that of failure.

Yes, Sergeant, he screamed in his head, back on that training ground.

Greyson pushed the door open on perfectly silent hinges and aimed his nerve scrambler at the well-lit emptiness beyond.

Nobody jumped out. None of them would ever move again.

Greyson stepped into the well-lit room and re-holstered his nerve scrambler. The pocket flash went in a moment later and the hand came out with a short stiletto he used more as a tool than a blade.

This was the first place he'd seen down here where every fixture was on. Greyson assumed an alien generator of some sort, since there wasn't the hum or smell of an old-fashioned human one burning fuel.

The room itself was rectangular. Ceilings that felt low only because the room itself was so deep. That same concrete on all sides, unpainted gray that had stained over the decades and been scuffed with rust from metal shelves moved around.

More metal racks stood in long rows parallel to the room and perpendicular to Greyson standing at the high end. Four rows of them. Junk had been pushed to the back end of the room to make space towards the front.

Ethen counted the bodies on them. Seven, so a new one in the last ten days.

Thank God he had buried Greyson Leigh's body in a place nobody would ever find it. He could just see Rachel recognizing her dead partner in that group and putting the nerve scrambler to the back of his head.

Kelly Anne Nazarian was there, naked like the rest and deflated to a poor reflection of what she had been, except for the fake breasts added later and made out of silicon.

Valdis Pandev was as well.

An accountant Zaborra had taken when they first arrived and needed to change forms into something human in a hurry. The man's wife, who had briefly continued on as Ethen's mask.

Until Zaborra had sent him after Dominguez, and, failing that, Greyson Leigh.

Rachel moved past his frozen self and inspected the corpses.

"Who are these others?" she asked, after identifying the same two Ethen knew.

"Probably on our printout," Greyson whispered back. "That's what Phrenic do."

Rachel lifted Kelly's corpse just enough to confirm how little the woman weighed. She took pictures of all of them with her handheld and logged them for later. Other crimes to solve tomorrow.

Greyson closed the door behind him and moved deeper into the room, cop eyes catching all the details and cataloging them for value. There was a desk against the left wall, where a supervisor might have once filled out paperwork, perhaps. Two filing cabinets next to it that had once held critical business records, before mice or something had nested inside and eaten everything.

He could smell the ammonia of their pee from here, even with the drawer closed.

Valdis wouldn't notice it. Greyson Leigh had always had a nose like a blood hound.

Trash in the can next to the desk showed where Valdis ate his dinner in the middle of the night. There was no place to refrigerate things, so he would sleep until mid-morning and then head out for fuel and coffee.

If you weren't paying rent or for a lazy girlfriend, your expenses went way down, since a Phrenic metabolism generally ran slower than human. Plus, if Valdis had killed recently, he'd be slowly digesting that person's blood and life.

Still, the man had a tendency towards Chinese food rather than Italian. Good to know.

Rachel joined him, taking more pictures of things.

"Got one that looks fresher than the others," she said.

Greyson let her lead him to the newest corpse. Four days dead, give or take, but he didn't know how he knew that.

Punk kid, maybe twenty years old from the thin face and wispy beard that hadn't grown in yet. Tattoos on neck, hands, and a bunch of other places normally covered with clothes. Nose that had been broken at least twice and not reset correctly either time.

A bully's face, even twisted in horror and frozen in death.

"This one looks less something," Rachel offered as they studied the young man.

"The most recently killed," Greyson said definitively. "Hasn't been completely drained yet, like Kelly or the others. He's still feeding on him. See the marks around the eyes?"

She nodded as Greyson touched the spots with the knife.

"Face tentacles go in through the orbital socket, but don't dislodge the eyeball," he noted clinically. "Leaves this kind of mark. I'd call it bruising, but that's not blood accumulated under the skin. Rather, it's digestive fluid that has worked its way in and is slowly dissolving the flesh."

"Yuck," she muttered.

"From the description, your killer had just started to do this to Dominguez when you surprised him," Greyson continued. "That's why it was hovering over his face like they had just kissed. They had, in a disgusting, kinky way. But he was starting to feed."

"I thought you didn't like Dominguez," she said abruptly. "Why are you so angry about it?"

"Cop-killer, Rachel," Greyson turned to look at her now. "Lowest of the low because they're going after the people who protect others. Even if Carlos was a worthless shit for the most part. He was still a cop."

"Oh…" she started to say.

Ethen heard the noise before Greyson or Rachel did. Caught the door opening out of the corner of Greyson's eyes, still silent as a tomb.

Saw Valdis standing there, home way too early, with a white paper bag slowly leaking steam from sealed containers.

Greyson Leigh's biological reflexes were better than either Phrenic's, but he wasn't here anymore. Just a guy pretending to look like Greyson. Sound like him.

Think like him.

Greyson would have been able to draw and shoot in time, but Ethen didn't have those skills.

Zaborra reacted in utter shock so brief that Ethen might have imagined it. Valdis dropped his dinner and reached into his jacket.

Greyson had been standing too close to Rachel, smelling her hair again. She wasn't tall enough to see over his shoulder and his body blocked her from watching the scene unfold, or she might have saved him.

Ethen shoved her hard with the fist holding the knife as Valdis pulled out a nerve scrambler and started to point it this way. Greyson reached for his as well, trying to dodge before Zaborra fired.

High noon.

Rachel stumbled and banged her head on one of the metal shelves before going down. Hopefully, he hadn't just killed her in his rush to get her away from the bolt that was about to kill him.

Valdis aimed almost as fast as Greyson did, because the cop still had that slightest edge, having somehow expected everything to go down this way.

Greyson threw himself to the side as Valdis fired. Pulled his own trigger before he had the target lined up.

Greyson Leigh felt the nerve scrambler take hold of his soul and dip it in acid. Every inch of skin was on fire. Distantly, he saw Valdis go to one knee, a hand holding the door frame, so maybe Greyson had given as well as he had gotten.

Except Greyson fell onto his face now, thrashing on the floor and Valdis had maybe gotten enough of the door in the way to block the bolt from killing him.

Still, both men had lost their pistols when they lost their minds.

Ethen screamed. Greyson didn't, but he was like that.

Calm, cool, tough. Everything Ethen had only ever dreamed of being.

Distantly, he heard Rachel stir. She had also dropped her nerve scrambler. Maybe a shelf unit had fallen on her. He wasn't sure what he had heard as he tried to save her life. If he hadn't just killed them both.

Ethen felt his body tear into pieces. His legs stopped being his and thrashed mindlessly. His arms did the same.

Somewhere, his heart stopped beating, and he was seconds from reverting to the base form that Rachel would find.

Hopefully, she would eventually forgive him.

Ethen's screams faded, but that was him losing control over his own meat, as well as his mind. Darkness closing in.

As he watched, Greyson Leigh turned around in their mind and faced him for the first time since the night Ethen had killed the man.

This wasn't the face in the mirror anymore. This was the best cop the Hunter Bureau had, just standing there, studying him with a dark, angry face.

Waiting for him to die.

Ethen wailed like a hungry child, because Zaborra would kill him, kill Rachel, and get away.

Ethen had failed.

"I can save us," Greyson said suddenly. "But you have to let me. You have to let go, Ethen."

Ethen stopped screaming. Stopped breathing.

Old nightmares washed up corpses and lost dreams onto the beach of his mind.

Deathwalker.

"No," Greyson shook his head. "I can't survive without you. But you won't live without me. Let go, and I can save us from Zaborra. I can save Rachel, and you'll get all the credit."

"You will," Ethen tried to say, but his mind was shutting

down. "I'm pretending to be you, because you're a better man than I am."

"Today, perhaps," Greyson nodded. "Tomorrow is your chance to change that. Just let go, Ethen."

Deathwalker, the greatest monsters of legend. Zombies feeding mindlessly until they failed.

But Ethen had no choice. He could die, or he could surrender.

He could simply stop being Ethen Boli, but hadn't that been his plan already? Try to continue to live as a better man than he had ever imagined he could be.

Do it, he whispered as the darkness engulfed him.

Greyson awoke from a nightmare so intense, so real, that he feared he might never close his eyes to sleep again.

Less than a second had passed. His nerve scrambler was still bouncing away from him where it had hit the concrete floor. Rachel was still falling, but she might already be out cold from where his push had been too wrong for her to recover.

And Zaborra was on one knee in the doorway, screaming just as mindlessly as Greyson had a moment ago. But that was the fear talking as Zaborra's eyes focused on him standing up and snarling.

Deathwalker, stepping out of the mist to come for your soul, you son of a bitch.

A nerve scrambler was spinning like a child's top between them on the cold, gray floor. Greyson staggered towards it as madness finally settled back into the eyes of a Baltic criminal.

Valdis squeezed the door frame and pulled himself upright. He spun drunkenly and lurched into motion away, trying to escape.

The man had a car out there. If Zaborra could just get far enough away, the nerve scrambler would lose its lethal kiss and the man could get into the metal safety of a rolling Faraday cage.

And then go find another victim and vanish forever, now that his former partner had turned on him.

Greyson took two steps and got painfully down on his knees to grab the gun, like the golden egg a magical goose had laid.

His hands didn't want to work right, but that was because they weren't really his hands. Weren't his eyes. Wasn't even really his soul.

Ethen wasn't dead, but was no longer the dominant personality in here. Greyson could hear echoes of others that had died and been taken, but he didn't have time to deal with all the theological implications right now.

Grab the gun. Okay, good.

He managed to get upright and fell towards the door, relying on Ethen's reflexes to keep the legs moving. Zaborra had vanished, but Greyson could still hear him, feet slapping heavily as if every stride was a challenge.

A race between two killers, both falling-down-drunk. It would be funny if it wasn't so damned deadly.

Out into the larger hall, hearing the outer door slam.

Greyson focused on all the things that old Drill Sergeant had pounded into him.

"They cannot defeat you, Leigh," the man had snarled one day. "They can only kill you, and that's ultimately a recognition of failure on their part. Remember that."

Yes, Sergeant, Greyson snarled back at the old man's ghost.

His legs still didn't want to work, but that was because they were really Ethen's legs, and he still had to get used to them.

Into the hallway, he listened both ways, looked both ways.

There.

Uphill.

He turned towards the parking lot and saw a shadow moving ahead of him, lurching just as badly as he was. But that would pass, too. The nerve scrambler hadn't hit either killer hard enough to do the job. In that, it was just an oversized palmstunner, a jolt of electricity from which even Zaborra would recover.

Greyson staggered after him, driving his killing need down into his thighs and feet, like the time his chute had failed and he had hit the jungle canopy hard enough to break bones, requiring him to walk with cracked vertebrae three days to an extraction zone.

You cannot beat me.

Darkness now. They were past the last of the working lights, but Greyson could still smell his prey, fleeing rather than trying to hide in the shadows and ambush him.

Zaborra's mind had gone all the way back to lizard brain. Pure, unconscious reflex that screamed *RUN.*

Greyson started to jog. Not that anyone else would call it that, but he sped up.

Hunter's High, even better than what a long distance runner got when they were into the zone.

Light like dawn suddenly. Zaborra had made it to the top of the stairs and was opening the hatch to escape.

Greyson snap-fired a shot, trusting thirty years of death-dealing to place it.

Zaborra didn't scream in response, so Greyson figured he'd missed.

Until a body came tumbling back down the stairs and slid to a halt at his feet.

Greyson knelt with only a few wobbles, and looked at the base form of Zaborra Strani. Because the Drill Sergeant said so, he shot the corpse again.

Never trust someone else's kill, or a shot into the dark.

The body didn't even twitch, but Greyson knew his kind better than that grizzled old killer in green had.

He drew a deep breath and tried to focus himself. Time might have passed. He wasn't sure.

Skin somewhere between human pink and concrete gray. Oversized eyes that would shrink as flesh moved around. Scutes protecting the sensitive spots like an upright pangolin.

A sound caused him to glance back.

Rachel had emerged, had her nerve scrambler centered on his chest as she stopped about twenty feet away.

Even through the light on the end of her pistol, he could see that she had death in her eyes, and one hell of a shiner starting to emerge on the right side of her face.

"Show me your hands," she ordered.

Greyson laid the nerve scrambler down carefully and put his hands in the air.

"Stand up," the order came.

Cop 101.

It took a little longer than he wanted, but he managed to get upright.

"Move away from the body."

He complied.

An hour ago, dying right now had sounded like the best way to solve everything.

But that was before. Greyson didn't feel like Jesus, but he didn't have a better way to explain it to the woman holding a gun on him.

Rachel picked up the nerve scrambler and stuffed it into a pocket. He wondered if she had been coherent enough to grab Greyson's weapon on her way by.

"You will bend down and very carefully removed the pistol on your ankle," she continued. "Slide it across the concrete and then sit over on the bottom stair. Am I clear?"

"You are," Greyson replied in a tired voice.

He didn't want to die. It would be stupid at this point. Pointless.

He moved like a half-broken old man, getting his pant leg up and putting the palmstunner down, but she didn't kill him, either.

Call it a win.

Rachel moved to the far side of the hallway, Zaborra's body between them. She knelt, from the way the light got lower, even with her gun still ready to snuff out Greyson Leigh.

"Greyson?" she asked, finally allowing herself something other than cop anger.

"Yeah," he said tiredly. "Thank you for not killing me."

"I had to be sure."

"I know," he nodded. "I had had a premonition that I wasn't going to survive the night, but his shot didn't get enough of me to matter. Sorry about your head. Was trying to save your life from a killer with a nerve scrambler."

"It's okay," her tone finally softened down to merely tool steel. "So this is base form Phrenic?"

"It is," he looked over at his old partner and didn't mourn. "If you take a deep sniff, they have a scent you'll never forget."

She did.

"Ew."

"Didn't say it was pleasant, but it gets into their clothes if they aren't careful about doing laundry regularly, so you might smell it again and know what caused it next time."

Always a cop.

"You okay?" she asked.

"Head's ringing," he admitted. "Everything hurts. Once the brass get here and take charge, I'm going to go home and drink enough of the synth whiskey that I can sleep without nightmares or pain."

"You aren't going to the hospital?" she asked.

No, I can never do that again. They might want to run a deep enough scan that they discover that I used to be Ethen Boli, before we became Greyson Leigh again.

"No," he muttered instead. "More cop magic. I'm so tough that I shrug off nerve scramblers like nothing."

"And what should I tell them about my face?" she followed, voice growing lighter and merrier. "Maybe the sex got a little rough and you had to punch me to help me get off?"

"Tell them the truth, Rachel," Greyson sagged as the adrenaline started to turn sour. "I panicked and threw you into a shelf, trying to shoot this miserable son of a bitch."

"Ya know, if you retire tomorrow, I can make up any story I want to," she teased.

Still, that light never moved from the pistol centered on his chest.

"Just be sure you want to be propositioned by people who like to hit girls," Greyson said as he took a deep breath. No broken ribs, but man it sure felt like there should be. "I need to call this in. You gonna shoot me?"

"You want to talk about walking nightmares?" Rachel's voice suddenly turned strange as he listened. "In my mind, I saw both of you as Phrenic for an instant. Like you flashed down to base form same as this punk, for just a moment when both of you fired."

Greyson went cold and still. She still had that nerve scrambler centered on his soul.

"Somebody went after Dominguez, but got away before I could finish him off," she continued, unwavering. "I wondered if maybe they'd been smart enough to go after the one man that everybody around the Bureau still considered the best. Taken Greyson Leigh next, before he knew that he had to watch out for a freak coming after him."

Greyson remained silent.

"But that would require there to be two of them, obviously, if I've got a dead one at my feet," Rachel's tones grew methodical. Cop voice. "And you said they don't normally work in pairs, unless one's utterly dominant and the other is submissive. Gas-lighting, you called it earlier tonight."

"That's right," Greyson agreed, wondering if he really had lost control of his form when Zaborra shot him, and hadn't realized it as Ethen died and let Greyson take charge.

She'd be sharp enough to catch details like that. It was what made her a hunter.

"So how would we prove that there weren't two of them?" Rachel asked casually.

"You could drag me downtown and find someone with the right hardware to do a scan," Greyson replied, wondering if even that might fail at this point, since he was Greyson Leigh genetically and Ethen Boli might no longer exist as an entity to be discovered even by that sort of a scan. He wasn't sure what they were now. "Or you could just shoot me right now and determine for yourself."

"You don't care?" she asked, just a little shocked.

"I'm tired, Rachel," he said. "I didn't want to come back, because I had a nice life and just wanted to go on being Greyson Leigh. I'm done with all the rest."

"All of it?" she asked, as if she could read his mind. "How?"

"This week has been educational for all of us," Greyson sucked in a shallow breath. "You learn things about yourself you never knew until you have to put your soul on the line."

"You've been a cop for a long while, and a soldier before that," her voice softened some.

"Yeah, but that was just my life I was negotiating with then." Greyson let down his guards inside as much as he could. His shoulders came down from his neck and the pain started to recede a little. "I've discovered some things I've been doing wrong my whole life, and now I have a chance to make things better. Make the galaxy better."

"By being a cop?" she asked.

There was a hesitation under her voice, like maybe she knew the truth, but hadn't decided how to act on it. Whether or not to just shoot him.

"By being the best cop I know how to be, Rachel," he said. "Stopping bad guys and helping teach a new generation of Hunters how to be even better than I ever was."

He waited.

She waited as well.

If death took him right now, at least Zaborra was done and would never kill again. Greyson might, but that would be because he was a cop and it was necessary.

No more feeding. Ever again.

The light wiggled and he realized she was removing it from her gun. She rested it on the bottom step and let it reflect off the ceiling and hatch overhead.

"Call Upkins," she ordered him in a casual tone. "Tell her the good news."

Greyson didn't have the energy to stand, so he just dug the handheld out and scrolled a little before pushing a button.

His eyes never left Rachel's.

"Leigh?" Denise was on the line before the second ring.

"It's done," he said, giving her the address for that strike team circling overhead, so that they could land hot in the grass nearby and take charge of things. "One dead Phrenic. Several bodies to identify so we can let the families know. A whole bunch of digging and backgrounding to follow, but it's done."

"You sound like hell, Greyson," her voice was warm and loving, like it had been back then. Before public and politics.

"It's been one hell of a week, Denise," he said. "A lot of things have changed, and I'm still getting used to them."

"Retiring tomorrow?" she asked.

He could hear the fear of it in her voice.

"No," he decided finally. "This guy's stopped, but the job goes on, if you want me to stay."

"My team will be there in three minutes, I'm assured by Edgar," she said. "And then we'll be there in twenty minutes to take charge."

"Yes, ma'am," he said and heard her hang up.

Greyson slid the handheld back into his pocket and pulled out some beef jerky to gnaw on. Wasn't as good as synth whiskey to calm the nerves, but it was all he had.

Rachel walked over and sat on the step next to him. He wondered if she was sniffing him, but he really didn't care. She'd kill him, or she'd accept him.

Either way, he won.

[18]

TOMORROW

G REYSON SAT ON HIS COUCH AND STUDIED THE caramel color of the liquid smoke in his highball glass. He'd considered buying himself an expensive bottle, but decided he'd grown too accustomed to the taste of the cheap stuff to do it justice. Especially since he'd left a thumbprint inside his glass at some point and not washed it wellenough.

One of the lights in here was on. Night had fallen outside.

True to her word, Denise's team had landed hot last night and almost professionally enough to impress him.

Almost.

But they were just gun bunnies for the most part. Rifles with legs attached, and not hunters. Not detectives.

Deadly enough, but they lacked *The Kill*.

Rachel hadn't shot him. Hadn't insisted he go to the hospital and get unmasked as the other Phrenic.

Or whatever the hell he was now.

Ethen had retreated into a tiny box, buried deep in their mind, like Christmas ornaments stored in a closet he no longer had. Just another one, in a long line of such boxes on that shelf, almost receding to infinity if he looked and sniffed hard enough.

True to his word, the man had let go. Seen the light, perhaps. Gone clean and sober, leaving Greyson the keys to the body and the instruction manual for how to drive it.

He understood where Deathwalkers came from now. A weak-willed Phrenic, like Ethen on a bad day, consuming a personality so strong that he couldn't control even the projection of the soul, let alone the whole person.

Like Greyson Leigh.

Eventually, he probably would have broken loose. Kicked Ethen out of their mind, and fallen into zombie mode. It required cooperation on both parts to exist as whatever they were now and not go down that path. That was why Phrenic generally moved on to weaker hosts as fast as they could.

Except Ethen couldn't do that. He had been forced by Zaborra to remain as Greyson Leigh until someone came along to prove their theory. Someone like Zielinski. Until Ethen and Zaborra both knew for sure that the cops wouldn't put their pettiness aside, wouldn't bring Leigh back from the cold and darkness.

Ethen had been required to subsume himself into the role of Greyson Leigh so deeply that he might never have escaped later. Until second thoughts led a career-criminal shape-shifter to have second thoughts about his life.

And Ethen had let go.

"Why?" Greyson fired the question into the darkness of his mind, like opening that closet door.

"You can make the world a better place, Greyson," the alien voice whispered back. "I would never have been able to do that."

Suicide by cop, then, in some bizarre manner. Taking monastic vows and hiding in a cave: poor, broke, and silent.

Do no more harm.

Greyson probed the man's memories. Read the knowledge that a Phrenic adventurer had accumulated over a life almost as long as a human cop. Greyson knew more about the species than probably any other being in existence now. Certainly, that would help him solve future crimes.

He studied the tiny ball of fear and shivering and sent a calming thought. Ethen had spent decades being gas-lit by various assholes. Zaborra had only been the most recent.

Battered spouse syndrome. Get them while they're still too young to know better and beat them into submission. Any sentient being can be broken that way.

Most never rise up and do something about it. Ethen Boli never would have, until he accidentally got his hands on a weapon named Greyson Leigh.

And then overcome his fear, at least long enough to stop Zaborra.

If Ethen had died in the process, he had still died proud. And enough of him had survived that Greyson could still talk to him, whenever Ethen wanted to emerge from his cave.

It might be decades before that man moved without fear.

A knock at the door as Greyson finished his glass, letting the warmth wash his soul clean as it went. He rested the highball silently on the end table and pulled the nerve scrambler from the holster under his arm.

He wondered how many months might pass before that wasn't his immediate reaction to strangers at his doorstep. Ethen had come in the window while he slept. Greyson had read the memories of how the man did it and fixed things to prevent the next burglar.

Greyson rose on silent, stockinged feet, ghosting across the old wooden floor and avoiding the squeaky parts.

Nobody carried slugthrowers anymore, but his training went bone deep. Greyson walked past the door as he approached, beyond the frame, and put a hand up to make the eyehole shadow.

"Who is it?" he bellowed through the solid wood panel.

A man standing outside might shoot a gun right now and put bullets through the head or chest of someone looking out. Greyson had killed two men that way, in another life.

"Rachel," her voice came back muffled. "I brought you something."

He leaned over and fisheyed her through the lens.

She was alone.

The nerve scrambler went back into the holster and he undid all the locks on the door.

Greyson considered only opening it enough to look through a crack, but he was too tired. A day of explaining things to the other detectives and typing up reports, broken up by a few catnaps and a lot of pain. Being too wound up now to even sleep was why he had been on the couch drinking.

That, and a fear of darkness.

"How'd you know I was awake?" he asked as he threw the door all the way open and studied the woman.

"Light's on," she smiled. "Saw it from the street."

She was back to cop. Gray slacks. Red shirt. Striped blue tie. Brown longcoat. One hell of a black eye. Box in her hands.

He was never doing a tie again.

Greyson turned and walked back into his flat, letting her follow. He grabbed a second highball glass after he retrieved his and poured her a finger for now. Without a thumbprint inside. She could get herself more if she was staying longer than two minutes.

Rachel rested the box on the table between them after she closed the door. It was about the size and shape of a shoebox.

Greyson just stared at the woman and handed her the emptier glass, waiting for her to start.

"Figured I owed you one," she finally said after taking a sip. A smile started to emerge around her edges. "After all the rough sex last night, and the soul-baring here in your apartment before we went hunting. And to apologize for nearly killing you."

"Always do what you think is right, Rachel," he said. "That's the most important thing I or anybody else can teach you."

"Understood," she nodded, lifting the lid and displaying a pair of cupcakes in a tray inside.

Greyson looked closely and someone had frosted them with *Happy Makeup Sex* in pink letters by hand.

His eyes rolled.

"After all the wild and tragic sex we had last night, I figured we should do more tonight," she said in a tone that he couldn't read.

Too tired.

Greyson retreated to the couch.

Twenty-five years younger and single.

And human. Because he wasn't.

Emmy was a different story, because she didn't want his soul, just his strength and calmness.

Rachel followed, glass in one hand and cupcake in the other. She sat as far away from him on the couch as possible, resting the glass on the other end table and carefully peeling her cupcake to nibble at.

Greyson stared at the woman and tried to put his thoughts in order. He hurt. He was half drunk. He was still trying to figure out how to explain what he was now to himself, let alone a relative stranger with a cute nose.

"Same sex we had last night?" he finally managed.

"Exactly the same," she nodded, breaking finally into a real smile. "Preferably with less bruising."

"Yeah, stupid move on my part," he said. "I panicked and tried to shove you clear."

"So he would just shoot you and I could kill him," Rachel turned serious again.

"Something like that," Greyson agreed and drank some more. "Then he did shoot me and I discovered that I wanted to survive after all. Wanted it more than anything."

"Should you see someone about it?" she asked.

"They'd just tell me I'm depressed and need to dig back to find out why," Greyson said. "I already know that answer, so I skipped all the other boring bits in between."

She waited, nibbling at the cupcake until it was already half-gone, but he wasn't going to fill in that chasm of silence with any of his secrets.

If she hadn't shot him last night, Greyson really didn't feel like giving her a reason to now.

"So now what?" she finally asked. "Where does Greyson Leigh go from here?"

He took a deep breath and let it go noisily.

"That's what I was trying to figure out when you knocked," he offered. "Denise has offered to keep me on. She also offered me the captaincy, but I told her what I thought of that idea. Cop I'm willing to consider, but not politician. Anything above Detective/Sergeant is a management gig. That's why I never pursued it."

"Didn't want to be a boss?"

"Twenty years in the army and I retired as a Master Sergeant, Asher," his voice got thin and sharp. "No interest in being an officer then. No interest in being a boss now."

"You just want to hunt bad guys," she offered.

"The world is filled with them," Greyson nodded, unsure how his glass got empty so quickly. He rose to refill it. "The aliens aren't generally any better or worse than the humans, and I happen to know more about some of them than anyone."

"Including the Phrenic," Rachel noted in a voice he categorized as *careful* while pouring. And smelling the frosting on the other cupcake.

"Especially the Phrenic," he replied. "Considering how many of them I've stopped over the last decade, it might be more than everyone else put together."

"And you're even better now," she added.

Greyson felt the world go cold again.

She knows the truth.

Cop instincts. There was a reason they made her a hunter. She didn't have all the training and experience yet, but you can't train *tall*, just like you can't train *killer*.

Greyson took his glass and returned to the couch.

Rachel Asher was studying him closely now. He'd say sniffing him, but there was none of that smell anywhere around him. Ethen had always been categorical about those sorts of things.

She wasn't pointing a nerve scrambler at him though. They were both without longcoats, so shoulder holsters were visible, but she'd have the advantage on a quick draw, since she was at that end of the couch and he'd have to draw all the way across his body.

"Why are you here, Rachel?" he asked in a deadly serious tone.

Happy Makeup Sex didn't cover it. There hadn't been any sex to begin with, other than the cover story to distract those two idiots from Vice who were currently unemployable anywhere that might ask background questions.

Just that shiner on her right side, like a raccoon had done half her makeup and then gotten bored and wandered off.

"Will I ever know the true Greyson Leigh?" she asked him.

Her eyes left very little doubt as to the layers of that question.

Who are you really? Was there a second freak, and he's sitting on the couch with me? Will you kill me, if we're alone and nobody might ever know the truth? Will you fuck me for real?

"Nobody will," he said after a pause to find whatever wisdom old age and treachery might have taught him. "I'm not the man I was two days ago. Or a week ago. Or a year. I'm not the guy that became a cop, or the one that became a soldier. I'll be someone else tomorrow, maybe. We'll have the same face and most of the same soul, but the answers I had when I was a civilian won't work when I go back to being a cop. That's another thing you'll hopefully learn from old farts like me before you make those same mistakes. As my mom used to say: It's okay to outgrow your friends. Or your old life."

"Same face, different soul?" she asked, sipping now at the whiskey, once the cupcake was gone.

"Best way I know to describe it, Rachel," he offered, almost out of words.

Waiting for her to draw her nerve scrambler and just finish him off. Put him out of his misery. Make sure that he would never slip and decide to kill again.

"Well, I suppose I'll have to keep you around for a while, then," she said in a light, almost playful tone that still went into his stomach like a knife. "There's too much I need to learn from you about how to be a better cop."

So he sat there until nearly dawn, telling her.

Blaze Ward writes science fiction in the Alexandria Station universe (Jessica Keller, The Science Officer, The Story Road, etc.) as well as several other science fiction universes, such as Star Dragon, the Dominion, and more. He also writes odd bits of high fantasy with swords and orcs. In addition, he is the Editor and Publisher of *Boundary Shock Quarterly Magazine*. You can find out more at his website www.blazeward.com, as well as Facebook, Goodreads, and other places.

Blaze's works are available as ebooks, paper, and audio, and can be found at a variety of online vendors. His newsletter comes out regularly, and you can also follow his blog on his website. He really enjoys interacting with fans, and looks forward to any and all questions—even ones about his books!

Never miss a release!

If you'd like to be notified of new releases, sign up for my newsletter.

http://www.blazeward.com/newsletter/

Buy More!

Did you know that you can buy directly from my website?

https://www.blazeward.com/shop/

Connect with Blaze!

Web: www.blazeward.com
Boundary Shock Quarterly (BSQ):
https://www.boundaryshockquarterly.com/

Knotted Road Press fiction specializes in dynamic writing set in mysterious, exotic locations.

Knotted Road Press non–fiction publishes autobiographies, business books, cookbooks, and how–to books with unique voices.

Knotted Road Press creates DRM–free ebooks as well as high–quality print books for readers around the world.

With authors in a variety of genres including literary, poetry, mystery, fantasy, and science fiction, Knotted Road Press has something for everyone.

Knotted Road Press
www.KnottedRoadPress.com

www.ingramcontent.com/pod-product-compliance
Lightning Source LLC
Chambersburg PA
CBHW070540100726
47907CB00004B/1202